The Adventures of Mountain Ma'am

I0521446

JULIANA REW

Cover Art by Keely Rew

The Adventures of Mountain Ma'am

By Juliana Rew

Discover other titles by Juliana Rew:

Erenarch Academy: Under the Dragon Banner
Miranda of Daris
Daris Moon
Mountain Ma'am

Cover: Keely Rew

www.julianarew.com

Dedication

This book is dedicated to my mother, Opal Marie Williams, who taught me to love my home state of Colorado and to appreciate the blue skies and white peaks of the Front Range.

*****~~~~~*****

Contents

*****~~~~~****

Introduction

Some might ask why "The Adventures of Mountain Ma'am" isn't a novel. That's a valid question. The fictional experiences of Callie Lock/Wellborn (née Dawson) are filled with Colorado names and dates and would easily lend themselves to a historical fantasy novel.

However, I've decided to write Callie's story as a series of linked events, often referred to as a "short story cycle." I was first exposed to the idea when reading Charles Stross's *Accelerando,* an ambitious and far-reaching science fiction family saga.

A cycle is a collection of short stories, yes, but in which the narratives are specifically composed and arranged with the goal of creating an enhanced or different experience when reading the group as a whole as opposed to its individual parts.

Wikipedia notes that short story cycles are different from novels, because the parts that would make up the chapters can all stand alone as a short story, each containing a beginning, middle, and end. Some of these stories were previously published in anthologies, so originally meant to have a "single effect." Still, as a group, the stories recount the changes Callie and her environment undergo over time and remark on the conflict between two opposing interests occurring throughout. In the case of the "Mountain Ma'am," this tension revolves around the interaction of humans and other animals in Nature.

Through both victories and setbacks, Callie processes each experience and ultimately creates her own destiny as a woman and as a steward of the environment.

*****~~~~~*****

Juliana Rew

Mountain Ma'am

I've got a Sharps rifle, and my best friend's a wolf. That's thanks to my husband, Harry. Best not to hang around when someone's out to kill you.

His parents were from Boston, but they had come out West to Colorado Territory after the Civil War looking to make a fortune on minerals and coal mining. So Harry was raised all hoity-toity, whereas I was brought up in Central City by a couple of miners who had found me cryin' my lungs out next to my dead mother. (I do cry a lot, but hell, I'm jist a female.)

Nobody would say Frank and Jess were great fathers; they mostly drank up any money they made from mining, but they did the best they could, I s'pose. They told me they thought I might be from West Virginia, since my nappies had a little flag of the new state sewn in.

They took me over to the schoolmarm, and she gave me some storybooks so's I could learn to read a little. I was at best a middlin' student, though, and as soon as I could I got a job at the Teller House sweeping out the dirt and cowdung that fell off everyone's boots.

It wasn't hard work, so I usually snuck next door to the saloon. My real teacher in those days was Kitty, the singer. I didn't know exactly what her job was, but she was real glamorous. When she sang, she traipsed all around the room, her ruffled skirt revealing tempting glimpses of her long legs. If anyone misbehaved, she gave them a piece of her mind. I knew she had a kind heart, though, 'cause she was always picking up stray animals.

In due course, my husband rode into town and found his way into the saloon. I was leaning on a broom and humming "Poor Little Liza" along with the piano player while Kitty took a break. I didn't notice him at first, but he apparently espied me, asking, "Hey, barkeep, who is that pretty girl?"

"Oh, that's Jess and Frank's girl. She's an orphan, you know. She ain't been good for much, but we've got her cleaning and baking, so's she's not a fruitless cause."

I overheard the tail end of this conversation and chipped in, "Don't forget I play the banjo, Blackie." I could play and sing a few of them sad tunes like "Falls of Richmond" and "Cold Frosty Morning." I had to borrow the banjo, though.

Harry began turtle-doving me right off. From the books, I had learned how ladies talk and how to do my hair in long braids like Rowena in *Ivanhoe.*

Kitty warned me about Harry. She fixed me with her green eyes and said, "He's no good, girl." She hissed whenever he walked by in the saloon. But I was star-struck by his fancy clothes and bowler hat. We got married in Idaho Springs and lived happily all through the next summer.

But those north winds began to blow, and snow began to stick on the rocks. The waterfalls froze into place, and the water mills stopped turning. Harry wanted me to stay home and cook him breakfast and supper on the fine Franklin stove he owned, while he went off and played Faro at the saloon. That was nice, but I didn't have enough to do except read, and I got restless.

Harry got home one afternoon about four as the sun was setting and didn't find me there. When I came in the door, he was sitting in the rocker in the parlor with a switch in his hand. I was real surprised when he laid into me the first time, but it became more common as the winter settled in. I would go out; he would punish me.

As spring returned, I took my usual forbidden walk up on the mountain. I saw an eagle couple roosting on the high crags. I knew they mated for life, and I knew I hadn't.

Harry had tried to keep me from roaming by taking my boots, but I made some up out of buffalo hide. Frank and Jess had given us a grizzly bear rug as a wedding gift, and that made a fine overcoat. In the middle of a fierce March snowstorm, I resolved to set out for good. Harry said if I didn't behave he'd shoot me with his father's old Colt .44, so I decided to take that with me.

He wasn't back from the Teller saloon yet, so I tucked his guns into my belt, along with a dozen bullets and a Barlow knife. I threw the lantern on the floor and watched the flames begin to lick at the carpet. The burning house put out a warm glow, and looking back I enjoyed the view until the swirling storm totally obscured it.

It was a hard and heavy climb, but I finally trudged my way over to Tennessee Pass by Leadville. That was a couple of counties away, and so high I knew that Harry'd never follow me.

In the morning it began to dawn that in my haste to escape, I hadn't thought this through very well. I had no money and no place to live. The rising sun shone so bright on the new fallen snow that it made my eyes sore, and the tears flowed down. I felt truly alone.

I heard a hiss and whirled around. I could have swore that it was Kitty with an "I told you so." No, only a bobcat high-tailing it away on snowshoe paws. Unless I miss my guess, it was Tewa, who was the first of many members of the Laramide Nation I was to meet. They call themselves the Laramide Nation, or sometimes "the Uplifted."

My stomach reminded me that it expected a bit of breakfast. I spotted an array of tracks in the turkey foot grass poking out of the fresh drifts. I fashioned the leather string I was using as a belt for the grizzly coat into a snare. I hung it next to a bush and bent down a springy branch as a trigger, then wandered off to look for a more permanent shelter. I hoped that I could remember this place when I wanted to return.

I didn't eat much that day. Spring was the worst time to find forage. Everything had been dead for months, and any berries had been picked clean by birds. I was lucky to find a few leaves of winterfat, and the furry silver sage leaves soothed my pangs a bit.

Although I was brought up by miners, women in the mines were bad luck, and the silver mines around Leadville were playing out, so I needed to look for other work. I thought perhaps I'd try my hand at fur trapping. While I did eventually catch a few pore critters, I felt sorry for them—and guilty—have you ever heard a rabbit scream? But I ended up eating most of what I caught.

The meager stash of pelts was hardly enough to wrap around my neck, and I was slowly starving. The bright Hunger Moon of March shone with a terrible beauty on the white peaks above the high park. Much as I loved the mountains, I was about to give up and crawl like a beggar down to town, when I spotted an elk. My shot echoed off the peaks. The elk stumbled and ran a few yards, but then fell. Maybe I could make a go of it after all. I ran up to it and knelt, but was stunned when I heard a voice!

It is an honor to save you, Mountain Ma'am. I shook my head in dismay and re-cocked the Sharps, but he had passed on. Lack of vittles and shelter had got me hearing things.

I had seen a cave earlier that month but was afraid to venture in. It was time for the bears to be waking up, and I didn't want to end up killed by one. Nights out in the open were filled with scary noises. Did you know nighthawks make as much noise as an angry buffalo? I screwed up my courage and lit a torch to see if there was anything wild in there. I was much relieved when I found it empty. It was big enough to camp in, and I could disguise it a bit with some brush.

I dragged my elk to the cave, all the time puzzling over what I might have heard, and carved out some meat as best I could. It was going to be good to have a permanent fire pit. I spitted some chunks on small branches and turned them over the fire. Surely some delicious elk would keep me from getting the Spring Sickness.

I was concentrating real hard on the cookfire when I heard a growl. I cursed, thinking it was a bear. But when I looked around, I discovered it was a wolf. A she-wolf, by the looks of her. This wasn't much better than a bear, of course. Wolves were known to travel in pairs, or even packs.

I kept my face to her and yelled, "Scat! Scoot, you hear? Get out of here!" I flung some clods of dirt at her, but missed. My hands shook pretty bad.

She stood there a while staring at me, and finally turned around and loped off.

I tried to stay awake all night to guard my elk meat, but I'm sure I dozed off a few times. The next morning I was dog tired, you might say.

I peered out of the cave, and there was no wolf in sight. To be on the safer side, I buried the leftover meat inside the cave and gathered the hooves and head to take down the hill a far bit—about a mile. I washed my face and hands in a cold stream to get some of the stink of blood off.

When I returned, the wolf was back. She began bounding at me through the trees. I froze, considering my options. I was wrestling the .44 out of my belt when she skidded to a halt and sat right in front of me.

Welcome, Mountain Ma'am, she seemed to say. The wolf was positively grinning, her white, daggerlike teeth surrounding a long, pink tongue.

That was not the option I was expecting.

Kitty told us you would be coming. The wolf simply sat there panting, but I could clearly hear her low, rasping voice.

"Kitty? From-the-saloon Kitty? Who *are* you?" I blurted. Here I was, talking to a wolf. Maybe I regretted not splashing a little more cold water on my face back at the stream.

We are the Uplifted. We are many. I am Sina, head of the Sawatch Range Tribe.

"The. . . Sawatch Tribe?"

Yes, this is our range. The mountains are ancient, and there are many tribes.

"Why can I understand you? Have I gone crazy?"

Kitty is leader of the Front Range of the Laramide Nation. She said to expect you, Sina replied. *And no, I would rather you **not** touch my head,* she added, ducking away from my outstretched fingers.

So, while I reluctantly refrained from petting her soft nose, Sina silently explained the situation. Anybody passing by would'a thought I was tetched, sitting there acting like I was friends with a great big ole wolf. I learned that many people and animals were members of the Laramide Nation, and that people like me were rare until recently. Most of the humans of the Uplifted were Indians. They had kept a closer connection to the earth and their fellow critters. I could understand that.

"But I don't even know where I came from. How come I can hear animals? I'm definitely not an Indian," I said, looking down at my white, freckly hands.

Kitty says you are the leader of another range tribe, the Appalachians, Sina said.

"Me—the leader of the Appalachians? Not likely," I replied. I'd never even been there.

Yes, that was your origin, Sina averred. *Tewa has smelled your birth nest. You are of the mountains. You are the Mountain Ma'am.*

She meant the nappies I was wrapped with as an infant, I s'pose. And West Virginia is in the Appalachians, I'd heard. I'd been in the mountains so long, this was actually seeming to make sense.

"Yes, well, I'm sorry I've killed some rabbits and that elk," I said, feeling a prick of conscience.

They were honored to serve you, Mountain Ma'am. You can talk to the new humans. You will fight for the mountain tribes and bring the humans to our side.

Gradually I came to realize that I had to go back and act civilized. I began to feel ashamed to have run away.

When I walked down into Leadville, everybody stared at me. I guess I looked pretty rough, dressed in furs, with a rifle and a wolf at my heels.

A pretty lady stepped up to me and said, "Oh, you pore thing" and grabbed me by the arm. It was Kitty. I should've known. Sina vanished up the street and into the hills.

"I s'pose someone told you I'd be coming, right?" I said, only half-joking.

Kitty got me cleaned up and staked me enough to start my own hotel and saloon, the Lucky Lady, then went back to her job at the Teller in Central City. Before she left, she told me Harry was dead. She said Harry was accused of cheating at Faro and had beat a hasty retreat into a bad snowstorm that night in March. He had gotten himself trampled after his horse was spooked by a wildcat. Tewa? Maybe. He sure could get around. I always wonder if Kitty slipped Harry an extra card.

I hung the Sharps over the fireplace mantle in the Lucky Lady and made a good living and a name for myself. I even got elected to the Colorado House in '94. Some say I'm famous for preserving the wild high country of Colorado. Of course, knowin' people like Teddy Roosevelt has helped a whole heap. And the fight for the mountains never ends. I once had a big tussle with Harry's family over some mining rights and nearly got myself killed.

One day as I was sweeping off the porch of the Lucky Lady, I saw a good-looking feller in a shearling jacket coming my way down Harrison Street.

"Drink, mister?"

That turned out to be Johnny, the love of my life. He hails from Pennsylvania, in the Blue Ridge Mountains. Sina had told me he would be coming.

Sina ushered me into a world that I had no idea existed. For years, me and Johnny'd often get a yen to scamper around the hills and camp rough. I still dream of running shoeless through the snow and howlin' at the wind with Sina and Tewa. Though I love Johnny to pieces, I confess I miss the days I was like a Mountain Man, wandering and self-sufficient.

I'm too old to wander now, but I recently had the privilege of meeting Sina's great-great grandson, Smoke. He was down visiting from Wyoming, as there ain't any wolves now in Colorado. We agreed as how this ability to commune with critters may be dying out, and every day I fear we'll lose the battle with greedy folks who want to take away the home Nature gave us. But the love of the mountains remains strong. I'm off to make the acquaintance of a young Parks ranger from the Tenmile Range. Smoke and I are hopin' something fierce that she'll be the next Mountain Ma'am, holding up the light against this troublesome darkness.

*****~~~~~*****

Family Matters, aka Frank and Jesse

Prologue

Just a *little* rest. She shrugged out of her heavy backpack, careful not to disturb the sleeping infant, and set it by the side of the creek. A tiny head covered with a scant strawberry blond fuzz barely peeked from the top of the papoose-style carrier. The woman sat down heavily next to it.

Rowena Dawson had been walking for two months, ever since the carpetbaggers had invaded her West Virginia town from up north. The influx of strangers had made it impossible for her to conduct the business of the mountains in secret. One toothless upstart had even spread it around that she must be running a moonshine still and vowed to find where she had it hidden. She didn't understand why they had come to West Virginia. It was Yankee country and had recently been admitted to the Union. It didn't stop the scalawags from looking to take what they could from folks trying to recover from the war. Now she was uprooted as well, now that Ronnie was dead.

Rowena remembered how she tried to persuade her husband Ronnie against enlisting.

"You've already got plenty of duties taking care of the mountain folk," she said. "I can't do it all alone, what with the baby coming and all. Let some of the other humans fight this war."

"I've got a duty to do this too," Ronnie pointed out. "The sooner the war is over, the sooner the people and animals can get back to their normal lives."

Ronnie made it through the war, only to die from a case of lockjaw when he cut his foot on a hook he was using to pull a stump.

She sighed. He shouldn't have tried to be a farmer. They were mountain people. But as he lay there delirious, he'd made her promise to take the baby out West, to the Colorado Territory. After the long trek across the flat grassland prairies, seeing the mountains rise into the sky was like going home.

Rowena rested, watching the sunlight sparkling on the rushing stream. She was following it to a town called Central City. Blue spruces marched over the hillside nearby. She and Callie would start a new life here, if she could find the range leader in this area.

She pulled a bit of pemmican out of the bag at her waist and nibbled at it. She wasn't sure she was going to make it all the way. She'd shed a lot of weight on the trek, and she'd been losing blood, a little at a time, since the baby came. It was worrisome, she knew, because it could attract predators. She was pretty sure she could find her way out of any situation involving beasts, but it was better to be healthy and in a position of strength before facing any. Her royal status wouldn't count for much if she was weak and dying.

But she had forgotten to take into account the deadliest predator of all. She jumped when she heard a heavy footstep and reached for her knife. She cursed herself that she hadn't paid more attention, but she was tired, and the crick was so noisy she hadn't heard his approach.

"Care to share a little of that food, little ma'am?" asked a large skinny man dressed in filthy buckskins. His rifle pointed casually in her direction.

"I reckon I could spare a little," she said, stalling for time and cutting some pemmican with her knife. He stepped forward boldly. Her heart was beating much too fast, and black spots swam before her eyes. She fell over sideways and passed out, her arms reaching for her pack.

The man bent down and shook her a little, but she looked real pale. Dead maybe. He picked up her knife, which had a fancy carving of a mountain range on the handle, and put it in his pocket.

"Oh, hell, I wasn't goin' to hurt you," he said. But he was hungry, and she *had* offered. He reached into the pack to see if he could get some food—well to be honest, all the food—but drew back when a loud wail issued forth.

A baby. If that didn't beat all. He hadn't even noticed it. Well, there wasn't anything he could do for a baby, or for its mother, from the looks of her. He grabbed the small sack of provisions from her belt.

"It's a sore shame. This ain't no country for a woman and baby." He lost no time retreating through the brush back the way he had come.

The baby continued to cry, hungry. A bobcat that had been loitering in their vicinity heard the cries and cautiously crept to the riverbank to satisfy its thirst. It sniffed around the motionless woman and the shrieking infant, then it too disappeared off to the west.

The next morning, two miners on horseback came upon the scene. One pulled out his rifle. A young gray she-wolf lay next to the woman, warily watching their approach, while nearby a baby cried weakly. The wolf sprang up and ran away growling.

"Good God, Frank. I hope we got here in time." Jesse pulled out a flagon of cow's milk and soaked his bandana in it, running over to the baby to wring drops into her mouth. She stopped crying immediately and sucked greedily on the kerchief.

Frank stooped and put his ear next to the woman's chest. He shook his head, then folded the woman's hands across her chest and covered her face.

"Too bad. Let's get her buried. Kitty said you and me was to take the baby if she didn't make it."

Frank reholstered his Civil War Sharps rifle on the saddle and took out a short-handled shovel. When they were finished, they took off their hats and paid their respects to Rowena, the Lady from the Appalachian Range.

"We respectfully consign this Mountain Ma'am to the mountains whence she came and give thanks for her noble service." A forlorn howl echoed from the nearby ridge.

They turned toward Central City. Rowena had only been five miles away, as the crow flies. Or as the bobcat runs.

***

Frank and Jesse

That Sunday Frank and Jesse took me out fishing was my first inkling, although I didn't understand it then. We had some fine cutthroat trout in Clear Creek, and Frank and Jesse said they knew about a deep hole where some big ones hung out. We trudged for about an hour to the spot, being careful to avoid poorly covered mineshafts, and set out our lines. Frank had twisted some hooks out of barbed wire, and we carried tin cans of worms we dug up in the yard back of the house.

We brought some corn muffins we'd bought from the Teller House and settled in for a long wait. Finally, I felt a tug on my line.

"Pull it in steady," Frank said. "Don't let 'im break your line."

I got excited, and pulled hard. Suddenly a giant trout that must have been six pounds leaped into the air, the hook caught in its mouth.

He rose to my eye level and looked me in the eye. I swear. He was ready for me to eat him if I wanted to.

All at once I didn't feel so good about killing this pore critter, and I threw the pole down.

"What the tarnation did you do that for," Frank yelled. "You almost had him."

"I—I didn't want to kill him, even though I felt like he gave me permission," I said.

"Ain't that what fishin' is for?" Frank said.

"Now, Frank," Jesse said. "You know she can't do what she can't do."

"Yes, but that was going to be dinner." Frank swore a little and looked over at me. Then he cooled off and reeled in the line, which had come loose.

Before I could ask if it wasn't strange to have a fish talk to you, Jesse steered the conversation away, joking, "Well, just think of this as the biggest fish story about the one that got away you ever heard."

I was a little sheepish about letting dinner swim away, but soon we were all laughing again. I was still a babe in the woods, and they were my pa's.

I didn't ever tell you about my stepfathers, did I? They were some devil's luck miners, let me tell you. They mined for all sorts of ore around Central City, Colorado—whatever hadn't played out yet—and they jist barely managed to put some food on the table. But they loved me.

Since I saw nobody else had two fathers, that's how I knew I was adopted. Frank Beinn and Jesse Northridge did what they could to keep me in nappies, and tore up strips of denim and homespun to the same pattern they found me wearing when I was a baby. They saved the original diaper, which had a flag of West Virginia sewn in.

Once I was old enough, Frank and Jesse sent me over to the school to learn to read, and after school I'd go to the Teller House saloon to sweep up after the midday meal they served.

It didn't seem to me as a little child like Frank and Jesse had much interest in being fathers, but I was always glad that they'd decided to pick me up that day in 1867 and take me into Central City. The biggest excitement we'd had was in 1874, when most of the town burned down. But it was rebuilt quickly, especially the saloon, and in 1878, the new opera house. When I got to be a woman, most times when I had a question about something, Frank and Jesse'd tell me to go ask Kitty over at the Teller House saloon. They said she knew more about female things.

Kitty Furtado managed the saloon and sang beautiful songs while sashaying around a little stage by the piano. Mostly that happened after I'd been sent home, but I snuck back over there one evening to see the saloon in all its nighttime glory, all lit up like a firefly. The men were all lit up too.

I was glad that Frank and Jesse didn't keep close watch on me, because I liked to wander around through the hills. I was a little restless, and it felt like I should be looking for something that was coming around the bend soon. I later found out that they knew all the time where I was going, and they knew why.

Sometimes the teacher would tell my fathers that I hadn't showed up for school that day, and they would always promise I'd be in the next day. That went on for a few years, until I said I wasn't much of a student and could read books on my own, and asked could I please drop out of school. This was fine with them as long as I did my afternoon job and brought home my fifty cents a week.

Kitty never let me lean on a broom very long.

"If you're looking for something to do, you could haul this pile of laundry over to the Chinaman, Callie. And don't linger too long on the way back."

"Yes, ma'am."

"And don't pick up any stray animals, hear?"

"Yes, ma'am." But I wasn't the one picking them up. She was. I kept asking her for a puppy or a stray dog, but she said Frank and Jesse wouldn't allow it.

"It'd probably end up dead, anyway," she said. I later learned that she meant Sina wouldn't allow it. Sina was a whole lot better than a puppy.

I never could afford to buy much of anything, but I appreciated the finer things in life, like Kitty's music. All the money we had went to the general store for food and supplies. Kitty saw me eyeing a banjo someone had pawned there and told me I could borrow the one at the saloon if I was real careful. I was in heaven learning all the tunes and playing along with the piano player when Kitty would let me.

My favorite was "Liza Jane," the part where she said, "I got a beau, you ain't got none. . ." I was beginning to wish I had a beau.

Along about the summer of my fifteenth year, Frank and Jesse and me were out gathering raspberries.

"Let's get goin' before the bears get 'em all," Frank said, handing me a bucket. "I got an especially sweet tooth for raspberries."

"My books say they are the queen of fruits," Jesse piped in.

"I don't know about that," Frank said, "I jist know I'm gonna get some cream at the general store and have me a big bowlful."

We picked until our fingers were sore from pulling the berries off the prickly bushes, even though we tried to be careful.

Jesse and I took a little break, and he asked me, "Are you reading your books, Callie? We said you could take off school, but only if you keep up with the reading."

"Sure, Jesse," I reassured him. "I'm reading that book you gave me called *Ivanhoe,* with this Lady Rowena. She's really brave."

"Lady Rowena, huh?" Jesse said, looking sidelong at Frank.

"You can learn about plants and animals and all from the books too," he said. "And I can teach you some about it too."

It was a good thing Jesse had so many books. We didn't have any kind of library until the 1900s, when this Scottish fellow Carnegie helped build a lot of them.

I was about to thank Jesse when we heard a crunching nearby, along with the sounds of bushes being scraped bare.

I mean bear. That's what it was, and it was right in front of us.

"Frank!" Jesse called. "Did you bring the Sharps?"

"No, I didn't think to," Frank said in dismay. He must have been particularly upset, because he'd once shot a grizzly and had the rug on the floor to show for it.

The brown bear rose on his legs and snarled, jist as startled as we were in what we'd found in the raspberry bushes.

Then he seemed to notice me and came down on all four legs. Jesse moved in front of me to protect me as best he could. But the bear began to circle us, looking at me keenly. Then he turned and loped off.

"Did you see that, Jesse? I thought he was goin' to attack us, but he decided he liked me and left us alone."

"That's right, child," Jesse said. "Let's get on home and get some of that cream Frank's been going on about."

Later that night, Jesse and Frank were talking when they thought I couldn't hear.

"It's happening, Frank," Jesse was saying. "She's got control over them now."

"Well, keep quiet about it. She's too young to handle it right now."

"All right. I'll try. But she's growed up. She's going to find out soon."

I wondered what they were talking about. What was I going to find out?

Well, one thing I was going to find out about was how to get married.

That spring Harry came into the Teller House. I didn't notice the fancy-dressed dude with the bowler hat at first, but then I heard him ask,

"Hey barkeep, who's that pretty girl?"

"Oh, that's Jess and Frank's girl. She's an orphan, you know. She ain't been good for much, but we've got her cleaning and baking, so's she's not a fruitless cause."

I chipped in, "Don't forget I play the banjo, Blackie."

Harry began turtle-doving me right off. At last I had a beau! Kitty didn't like him, though. She hissed whenever he walked by in the saloon and warned me, "He's no good, girl."

I could sort of tell that. He did seem kind of dangerous. He carried a .44 and ordered everybody around, including me. But I was so star-struck I didn't ask questions. He popped the question, and I said yes right away.

I ran home to tell Frank and Jesse, and was crushed when they said no. They said I was too young, and besides, they didn't know anything about this fellow.

I was crying when I told Harry that I couldn't marry him. I wanted to get married so bad I could taste it.

"Don't worry, Callie," he said. "My father's coming to town, and he'll fix things."

The next week Harry's father arrived in Central City. He turned out to be Zachariah Lock, the famous mining mogul, arrived recently from the East to make his fortune on minerals and coal as America rebuilt itself following the War.

Harry introduced me to his father, saying "Callie, may I present my father, Zachariah Lock. Callie, this is my father."

Well, Harry was wrong about his father fixing things. Old Zachariah took an instant dislike to me and me to him. He was cold, and the look in his eyes told me he thought I wasn't good enough for his precious son. Harry had been raised all hoity-toity, whereas I was only a worthless orphan girl.

I heard them arguing at the corner table of the saloon.

"You'll not marry that girl, or I will disown you!" old Lock was saying.

"I'll do as I please," Harry retorted.

"What will you do for money?" his father said.

"I know how to make money," Harry said. He didn't mention that his way of making money was gambling at Faro in the saloon. He was little more than a card shark.

Later Zachariah followed me as I was cleaning rooms and pulled me aside.

"Young woman, you know you can't possibly marry my son. You're too young, and he can't possibly support you. What if you had children? They would all starve. Here, I can give you fifty dollars to break off the engagement. That's my final offer. Think of the things you could do with that much money. If you only leave Harry alone."

Fifty dollars was a princely sum in those days, but I had no interest in the money. I told him that I wouldn't take it and that we were going to get married, no matter what.

He grabbed my arm and squeezed it hard.

"You're hurting me." He took his time about letting me go. I hurried home after that, shaken.

It was hard to believe that Frank and Jesse felt the same way about me not getting married. They even

26

suggested I take the money from Lock. Well, I was even more insulted and said we were going to elope over to Idaho Springs even without their permission.

Reluctantly they agreed to sign the papers, and me and Harry got married. We moved into a little house in the hills above Central City. Harry's father cut him off, which I s'pose contributed to his heavy drinking, but we were determined to have our way.

Frank and Jesse came to the house to offer us wedding gifts, of their most precious possessions, it turned out. They gave us the big grizzly bear rug and the Sharps rifle Frank had carried during the War.

Harry wasn't that pleased to see them, and after dinner they got into an argument. Harry kicked them out, telling them not to come back.

"If he gives you any trouble, you call us, Callie, you hear?" Jesse called out as they were leaving.

Embarrassed, I agreed and hugged them goodbye. Harry slammed the door, and he and I were alone together at last. Well, I never was all that good figuring out people, and Harry was my first lesson to be more careful.

***

Best Laid Plans

Frank and Jesse stood outside the cabin.

"I don't feel good about this, Frank," Jesse said.

"I know, but we did what we could," Frank said. "It's not easy being a mountain guardian. No one would believe us. But we've taken care of a long line of Mountain Ma'ams and Men. We'll just have to go back to Kitty and ask what to do next."

"Yeah, that carpetbagger Harry is an unexpected complication. We need to know what to do until Callie's true mate gets here," Jesse said.

"Until then, it's best to soft-pedal this business about her and her animals. We ain't even sure if her mate has shook off that wolf curse yet. I hear tell he's mountain royalty too—and just as hard-headed as Callie."

###

*****~~~~*****

Raised by Wolves

He was bleeding from his snout, but he had to keep moving. The men had been lying in wait when he came to scout the dozing herd. There wasn't even time to pick out a weak calf before he heard a shout. He smelled the fear of the horses as the men yelled to each other. A deafening noise, the acrid reek of smoke, and the pain in his side all seemed to happen at once. Confused, he set to running in the direction of the full moon as it sank on the horizon.

More explosions sounded over his head as he panted for air. There was little cover out here on the prairie, but at last he reached a small sandhill bluff covered in tall grass and crawled in on his belly. He would lick his wound and wait. Maybe the men would go away. They continued to circle while he shivered in the dark, emaciated and exhausted. Another night of dumb misery.

***

He awoke at sunrise, rolling over to stare upward at the plumed grass that had served as his canopy. Light sparkled through the reddish blades, warming his face. A meadowlark was whistling on a marker post nearby.

"Yeah, yeah. Shut up, will you?"

He sat up to check that he was all in one piece, and winced as his fingers probed his cheek. He must have gotten cut last night somehow, but it was already healing. He never could remember what happened to him at night. Every morning he faced the humiliating task of finding some clothes and staying out of the hands of the locals for whatever had transpired the previous night.

His uncle Matthew Wellborn was somehow punishing him for refusing to do his bidding. But Johnny didn't want to marry this complete stranger out West in Colorado, strictly in the name of duty.

"I'm perfectly comfortable here at home in Pennsylvania, Uncle," Johnny had said. He stood in the forest outside the family's farm practicing for the mountain tournament. Everybody knew he was a shoo-in for the archery title. He brushed back a lock of blond hair and absent-mindedly reached into his quiver for another arrow. He knocked it in his bow and took aim at a tiny glass bottle he had set upon a log about 50 yards away. His uncle Matthew could barely make out the little target; only the glint of the sun on the gold stopper revealed its presence at that distance. Johnny loosed the arrow, and Matthew heard the clink of breaking glass.

"Nice shot. But you've got to go," Matthew said. "We've promised."

"I don't see why I should have to do it," Johnny said. "Now that father's gone, I'm next in line as head of the Blue Ridge Mountain Tribe, soon's I turn 18. Why don't you send Seth?" Seth was his younger brother.

"Seth's not old enough to go, and besides, it has to be the leader," Matthew said. "What's holding you here? You could be leader there just as well, and the alliance with Callie Dawson would align two powerful Tribes."

Johnny already had plenty of gals to keep him company in Pennsylvania. Take Miss Mary Ellen, for example. She brought him blueberry pies and other gifts fit for a king, which is what he already was. He shouldn't have to take orders from anyone. Plus, things were a lot more civilized here.

Uncle Matthew had sighed and explained it all over again to him. His brother Seth was going to head the Blue Ridge as Regent, and Johnny was to go mate with the Appalachian Mountain Ma'am out in Colorado. That was the agreement they'd made with the wolves.

"Humans are killing wolves at a high rate, and the Laramide wolves need our protection," Uncle Matthew said.

"Wolves are all fine and dandy, but I'm not interested, Uncle," Johnny said. "I've got plenty to keep me busy here."

"You've been chosen to represent the alliance, and you damned well will keep the bargain," Matthew retorted. "We owe our very existence to the wolves, going way back. When are you going to do something with your life, Johnny?" Matthew spluttered.

Johnny didn't know. He only knew this wasn't his idea. He kept refusing his uncle's entreaties, until finally one day Uncle Matthew lost his temper and all *this* started happening. . .

He was out on the prairie somewhere, that was evident. Buck naked and in a different place every day. He began walking, looking over his shoulder constantly. After an hour or so of casting about, he spied a small farmhouse. A curl of smoke rose from the chimney. Ah, some luck. Laundry hung out to dry would obscure his approach. He pulled a sheet off the line and wrapped it around his waist, climbing barefoot up the wood steps onto the porch.

He rapped on the door and called out.

"Hello. I'm sorry to bother you, but I'm lost, and I'm hoping you can help me." He knocked again.

A long silence followed, but at last he heard a latch pull. A rifle barrel peeked out at him. A woman's voice hollered, "What d'you want? I'm warning you—I'll shoot if ya try anythin'!"

He put one of his hands up. He kept holding the sheet with the other.

"My name's Johnny, ma'am. I'm from Pennsylvania. I've lost my way, and I need help getting home. Can you tell me where I am?"

"Yer in Nebraska, ya fool. Hey, what are ya doin' with my sheet? I jest washed it."

"I've lost my clothes. Robbed, I think—I can't remember."

"A likely story. Probably out drinkin' and carousin', I'll wager."

"I'm not sure. Can you help me?"

The woman let him in, eyeing him up and down. Johnny knew he looked a sight and shifted from foot to foot. She put down the rifle and tied on an apron.

"Set down, and I'll get ya some biscuits and coffee," she said. "You need to put some meat on your bones."

"Are you all alone here?" Johnny asked.

"What business is that of yours? My husband's in town and will be back tonight."

"Well, could I borrow some of his clothes so I could go into town?"

"All right, but you've got to give them back. Leave them with Tom Holden in the general store. Say they're for Jack Terry."

Johnny thanked her and asked her name.

"I'm Anna Terry, and if you don't give them clothes back, we'll hunt ya down, ya young idiot." It wasn't the first time he'd been called that.

Wearing actual clothes and well breakfasted, Johnny headed west in the direction Anna pointed. She said they didn't allow a lot of fences out here, so it was hard to keep a straight line, but he kept the sun to his left. A little after noon, he came upon a sorry excuse for a town, but at least it had a general store.

He walked in. The store had meager supplies—a few sacks of flour, some beans, and coffee. He didn't see any clothes for sale.

"Hello, sir. Is there any chance I could do some chores for you so I could buy a meal and some clothes?"

"What's wrong with the ones you're wearing?"

"I just borrowed them from Jack Terry. Are you Tom Holden? I'm s'posed to give them back to you."

"I could use the help," Tom said. "My lumbago is bothering me something awful." He handed Johnny a broom and offered him 10 cents a day to help out. Johnny put all his energy into sweeping the store and making himself useful.

"Would it be okay if I stayed overnight?"

Tom allowed as how he'd been a good worker and pointed him to the spare storeroom in the back, which was nearly empty.

"We used to salt and brine beef in there, but the cowboys say the dang wolves have been cleaning out their longhorns. Nobody wants to butcher a steer that's already been torn to shreds and left to the flies."

Johnny shivered at the thought of men out hunting the wolves to extinction. That night, he braced the door shut with a wooden 2x4 and folded his newly bought clothes in a stack in the corner. He wasn't going anywhere until he found out what was going on.

The next morning Tom asked him if he'd had a restless night.

"I kept hearing thuds and stomping. I heard some of them wolves howlin' too, so I din't get any sleep last night," Tom added.

Johnny apologized and said he was a sleepwalker, so he had to lock himself in, which seemed to satisfy Tom.

Johnny worked for a week and a half, saving a few pennies each day, and went to the telegraph office to send his uncle a message. It just said: AM IN NEBRASKA. WHAT HAPPENED?

He waited another couple of days, but there was no reply.

***

He couldn't see. This place looked and smelled familiar, like fear. He broke into a run. A horse whinnied, and a loud boom exploded. The barking of dogs was getting louder. His body hurt, and his paw left a smear where a toe had been torn by the trap. He ran until he was winded, then lay down, suffering silently. He might die, but he couldn't get up.

He heard the footsteps of a dog patter up behind him and tried to flatten himself. A long nose nudged him in the side. Not a dog. A she-wolf. He staggered to his feet and followed her. They found a gully, and she nipped at him with little snarls until he rolled in. She stood guard over him until morning.
***

Johnny awoke at daybreak, in time to see a big gray wolf with gold eyes staring down at him. She turned and ran off. He cursed, chastising himself for getting into this situation again. It was just that he was set on knowing what was happening to him at night, and yesterday afternoon he'd heard some cowboys in Tom's store talking about wolves. He'd risked going out to investigate.

The cowboys said they'd seen a big wolf bitch last night, but it wasn't the same one as before. That one had been a half-starved lone wolf. A couple of strangers listened with interest to the talk of wolves. The shorter one introduced himself as Jesse Northridge and said he was here with his partner Frank Beinn. They were miners, visiting from out West.

"Maybe she was looking for her mate. Wolves run in pairs or in packs, ya know," Tom said.

"We ain't seen the lone wolf for a long time," one cowboy replied. "Probably dead."

Johnny decided then that he had to take another chance and see if he could tell what the she-wolf was doing there. Maybe it was a message from his uncle.

Well, that hadn't turned out to be the case, and at any rate, he couldn't remember much of what happened last night. He limped home (what happened to his foot?) and snuck around the back of the store to try to slip into his room without being seen.

"Kind of cool for walking around in the altogether, ain't it?" Tom said. Johnny jumped.

"I— I guess I was sleepwalking again, Tom."

"Well, try to wear some long johns from now on. And keep your trap door shut. We can't have the town ladies having fainting fits."

"Yes, I'll do that. Thanks." Johnny slipped into his room and ran for his clothes.

Working for Tom wasn't so bad, and Johnny was glad to have a place to stay while he tried to reach his uncle. Tom had him put up another set of display shelves in the store for stocking canned goods. Johnny began running up and down the ladder, and Tom was in the middle of telling a joke, when two men came in. These were some rough-looking characters, even rougher than the visitors he'd seen yesterday. They hadn't seen so many customers in weeks.

Tom asked, "Help you boys with anything?"

"You got any more of this here cough elixir or fever tonic?" he said, picking up a bottle of evil looking liquid. "My friend's got a bad case of the ague." He shot a look at the second man, who hadn't been coughing before, but started up hacking and wheezing.

"Yeah, I might," Tom said. "Johnny, would you go in the back and look in my wardrobe closet?"

"Sure thing. I'll be right back," Johnny hopped off the ladder and ducked behind the curtain.

"On second thought," the first man said, "I think we'd rather take that money I seen you put in the till." He pulled his gun from the holster and pointed it at Tom. Tom put one hand up, and started to open the till with the other. Suddenly Johnny called out.

"Is this what you needed, Tom?" The robber spun around, only to see Johnny aiming a bow and arrow at him. The bottle in his hand shattered suddenly. Tom's mouth dropped open. The man raised his gun.

"Look out, Johnny!" Tom yelled. The robber's shot narrowly missed Johnny's head. Johnny calmly stepped to the side and aimed another arrow at the man's knee, which brought him down, howling in pain. His companion bolted for the door. He jumped on his horse and galloped away.

"What part of 'I'll be right back' didn't you understand?" Johnny said.

After the sheriff collected the robber and put him in what passed for the town jail, Tom turned to Johnny to thank him properly.

"I didn't know you were so good with a bow," he said. "I'd forgotten I even had one back there."

"Welcome, but sorry I broke your bottle of tonic," Johnny apologized.

"That ain't important," Tom said. "It feels good to have a young man in the store again to help take care of business."

***

Two mornings later, Johnny heard a knock. He pulled out the 2x4 and stuck it behind the door.

"Lady here to see you."

"Me?" Johnny wondered who it could be.

"Yeah, and real purty too. You been wearin' your long johns, ain't you?" Tom joked.

Could this be the Mountain Ma'am?

A tall woman dressed in a black dress and wearing red velvet shoes and a feathered hat introduced herself.

"Hello, Johnny. I'm Kitty Furtado. I live in Central City, Colorado Territory. Your uncle and the head of the Sawatch Range Tribe sent me to talk some sense into you. Your delaying is causing all sorts of problems. Sina told me you were here, and that you were a wolf, but she couldn't talk with you. Your uncle's curse must make you dumb.

"You know you make a piss-poor example of a wolf?" she continued. "Sina said they almost killed you, and you looked like you hadn't eaten in weeks. She had to force you into a bar ditch to hide."

Sina must have been that wolf he saw this morning, he thought.

"Are you the Mountain Ma'am?"

"Hell, no, she's a little slip of a thing. . . I might have a tintype of her in my saddlebag," Kitty offered. "Do you want to see what she looks like?"

"No, thanks." Johnny was pretty sure she must be ugly for all this fuss about getting her a mate.

Kitty must have read his thoughts.

"But she's already gone an' got herself married. You've got to come get her."

"If she's already married, why would I want to do that?"

"We'll take care of that. You just need to come, and Callie will be yours. She's your true mate. If you don't, the alliance will be broken, and you'll be a dumb animal the rest of your life. Just think about who you'd rather be."

Callie. Hearing that name stirred feelings deep inside him. Suddenly he knew he was destined to be at her side, whoever she was.

"I guess I *would* like to have a look at that tintype," he said. Kitty left and returned with a stiff metal plate wrapped in parchment. As he looked at the girl in the picture, she seemed to come to life and look directly at him. Although she wasn't smiling, it felt as though they shared a secret jest. He shook himself and handed it back to Kitty.

"I'll think about it," he told Kitty. She impaled him with piercing green eyes that held him like a frog on a spit.

"But hurry," she said. "Frank and Jesse and me can't stay here forever protecting your precious ass. And Sina's risking her life even being here."

"Who are Frank and Jesse? You mean them miners?" Johnny asked, confused.

"Never you mind. Just git. Time is short." Then she left.

A day later, a telegram arrived for him. It said: HAD ENOUGH?

After talking with Kitty, Johnny had finally figured out that his powerful magician uncle had cursed him to become a wolf at night, even if he couldn't remember most of it. Johnny wrote back: YOU WIN, UNCLE

That night, he folded his clothes as usual and waited for the nothingness to take him as it did every midnight. This time, though, nothing didn't happen, and when the sun came up the next morning, he remembered the whole night.

He dressed, walked around to the front of the store, and told Tom that he was leaving.

"I've learned a lot from you about the general store business, Tom, and I'm grateful, but I have business in Colorado and need to be moving on," Johnny said. Besides, that 2x4 holding the door was nothing but a toothpick now.

"I'm real sorry to see you go, boy. Um, could you wait a minute?" Tom asked. He left the store and came back with a heavy shearling jacket.

"It gets cold out there in Colorado," he said.

Johnny was speechless. This jacket was worth 10 dollars at least.

"It belonged to my son. He died in the War. You've been an honest boy, and you worked hard. I want you to have it.

"I forgot—Did you hear the news?" Tom added. "They found that it wasn't wolves killing the cattle. It was a pack of rustlers. Used to be Confederates in the Civil War, I heard. Remember them two strangers here in the store a couple of days ago? I know'd they was bounty hunters, even though they said they were miners from Colorado. They told the sheriff they'd tracked the rustlers down and wanted help arresting 'em."

Another lucky break, Johnny thought. Miss Kitty would be happy to hear I'm on my way and the wolf situation in western Nebraska has been solved. That she-wolf protectin' me was something, wasn't she? According to legend, Romulus and Remus, the founders of ancient Rome, were raised by wolves. 'A course, that was folklore. But there's always a grain of truth somewhere in those old tales.

Johnny shouldered his pack and set out on foot. He wasn't sure where Central City, Colorado Territory, was, but he was sure he'd find it in due course. Just keep heading west. All roads would lead to the Mountain Ma'am.

###

*****~~~~~*****

Skunks Versus Woodpeckers

Callie Lock tossed a bucket of dirty water out into the street of Leadville. She ran the Lucky Lady Boarding House and Saloon, and the chores were never-ending. Due to her husband's recent untimely death, she did it alone. She tasted a drop of salty sweat and wiped at her forehead.

"I sure could use some help around here," she said, bending to wring out the mop. It was hard to keep up, what with all the night patrols she had been doing lately. The end of summer was approaching, and humans and animals alike were busy preparing for the harsh winter sure to come.

As scion of the Mountain Ma'am for the Appalachian Range, she had been transported to the Rockies as an infant, and now that she was grown she handled human-animal relations hereabouts, though it had been a shock to learn that this responsibility fell on her 16-year-old shoulders.

"Fine way for royalty to get treated," she grumbled, grabbing a broom and sweeping off the boardwalk in front of the saloon. Her best friend and chief enforcer Sina the wolf had let on like she was some kind of queen of the mountains.

The air smelled faintly of skunk, and Callie wondered if one had taken up residence under the wooden porch. The pungent, musky aroma smelled kind of nice, actually, unless you were the recipient of a direct squirt.

The garden needed attention too. She was about to head back through the swinging doors to get her garden hoe, when she heard the distinctive rat-a-tat of a woodpecker, faster than a gatling gun. These hard-beaked fowl were valuable for eating insects out of the trees and carving out nesting places for other birds. Callie often listened for the news they brought. It was still a wonderment that she could understand bird talk—and not just trained mynah birds, either. This bird turned out to be a male flicker, fancy in a polka dot breast and red-striped head. Too bad the town's buildings were storefronts with wooden clapboard siding. This attracted the peckers away from the forest, where they should have stayed if they knew what was good for them.

It was kind of a coincidence seeing two nuisance species at one time here in town. Woodpeckers usually disappeared around July. Of course, they were only nuisance species to the human inhabitants, though it was hard to say which was worse, horrible smell or horrible noise.

"Get on out of here," she yelled, and waved her broom. The ruffled woodpecker shot her a disgruntled look and clumsily lifted his heavy body into the air with a piercing kee-ar and mighty flapping of his salmon wings.

She tapped her broom on the porch. "And that goes for you too, skunk. I know you're under there." Soon a fluffy black-and-white tail emerged and could be seen bouncing off toward the side street of the saloon.

As she watched the skunk's retreating behind from a safe distance, he glanced back, and she caught his angry thought, *We are at war with the woodpeckers.*

Feuding between polecats and woodpeckers. Now, that was the craziest thing she ever heard. Well, maybe not the craziest. . . Thinking you could understand what animals were thinking might be even crazier.

Skunks versus Woodpeckers

"Anyway, not my problem," she mumbled. At least it wasn't humans shooting ever' critter in sight, like usual. The mule deer were especially hard hit, as people laid in stores of venison for fall. And she'd heard a lot about the plight of the wolves from Sina.

Back to finishing up the chores. At least this would be a nice one. She cut through the kitchen to the back garden and began watering her tomatoes. She was growing them from seeds her stepfathers Jesse and Frank sent her from Central City. Her mouth positively drooled with the prospect of the good eating these tangy red beauties would provide in another week or two. After scuffing away a few weeds, she leaned on her hoe, soaking up the sun and listening to the bees as they worked a patch of clover nearby.

Her mind wandered back to skunks. She knew the little weasel-like critters were no friend of honeybees; the skunks' thick coats protected them as they scratched honey out of hives. What'd got them on the warpath with woodpeckers now? Messed up nests? Squabbles over food? Rabies—or distemper? Could birds even get rabies? Were they natural enemies? There was no way of telling what could have set them off.

***

As owner of the Lucky Lady, very little that people said or did escaped Callie's attention. The miners and loggers often came in for meals and a few drinks of the local solace. The Indians called it firewater, but they weren't allowed into the saloon. Cal liked to play banjo and entertain by singing popular tunes. She had a fine voice, if she did say so herself.

"Mr. Dexter is working us like all tarnation," Erasmus George said one day. "He's wanting us to get that logging road to the sawmill built 'afore the snow flies." Leadville was growing fast, and the demand for wood boards to build houses was expanding.

43

"I cain't work fast enough for 'im, 'cause some stupid bird tore into me," he complained, raising a bandaged hand. "Danged woodpeckers."

As she wiped the table next to him, Callie noticed an unmistakable scent. With his shaggy dark hair and white striped beard, Erasmus did look a little like a skunk, but now he smelled like one to boot.

"Where's this road, Erasmus?" Cal asked. The road was off her usual rounds, to the south of town. She would go look it over after closing.

Late that night Cal crept out of her rooms on the top floor of the boardinghouse and down the side stairs. She carried an old Sharps rifle and a .44 pistol she had stolen when she ran away from her husband. Lucky for her, he was dead now, caught cheating at cards in Central City. She sometimes wondered whether her friend Kitty at the Teller House might have dealt him that hand. Kitty had helped set her up as proprietor of the Lucky Lady here in Leadville.

Her near starvation and subsequent encounters with a wolf in the snow-covered mountains led Callie to believe she was the "Mountain Ma'am," ordained by Nature to see that humans took care of these mountains and their fellow animals.

The Green Corn Moon was rising as she set off on an easy jog toward Turquoise Lake. She again felt a little dissatisfied. She was young, so it wasn't that hard to do these patrols. But why was she here? It didn't seem like anything was happening that didn't happen before. Sure, people killed animals, but Sina had told her that was normal. Everyone's got to eat, after all. Now, what was up between skunks and woodpeckers trying to kill each other? Had a woodpecker attacked Erasmus because he smelled like the enemy?

She entered a clearing near the lake, a place she often went to think. The moon dimly lit the small patch of land surrounded by tall, almost black, conifers. Millions of tiny stars twinkled overhead. If she had been religious, she would have thought she was in a cathedral. She'd read about those in Jesse's books when she lived in Central City. She missed Jesse and her other stepfather Frank, but she had started a new life here in Leadville. She would send Jesse a note the next day and to ask him to send some books on skunks and woodpeckers. She wasn't sure why those kept pushing into her mind, but maybe it was a sign. *Or a job.* She was restless to do some real work, not just pack lunches for miners.

As she trudged through the forest to the top of the ridge, she could see that a lot of trees had already been felled. They lay waiting for the road to be finished so they could be dragged into town for sawing. At the edges of the manmade devastation, she saw trees that showed the telltale scaled bark of woodpeckers.

"Callie Dawson, ain't it?" She jumped. Not everyone knew her maiden name.

"Erasmus. What are you doing here?"

"When you asked about the logging road, I figgered you might come and take a look. I been puttin' in overtime trying to catch up. You're trespassin', you know."

"Is that so?" His musky smell seemed stronger than ever.

Cal tapped on the side of one of the trees. She could hear buzzing and crying noises. Baby woodpeckers. That wasn't right! They should be pretty much all grown up and heading south soon. A three-toed woodpecker fluttered out, uttering cries of distress. The bird's coat was a drab brown. Probably neither she nor her chicks were getting enough food. Without food, they wouldn't make the migration. *Not so cagey as flickers,* she thought. And a lot easier to scare than the flicker she'd seen in town. No surprise she hadn't seen any peckers in town. Suddenly, the mother bird screamed and dived, barely missing Erasmus. He ducked.

Out of the corner of her eye, Cal noticed movement. It was the white markings of more skunks, approaching in a pack. This wasn't right either! Skunks didn't usually travel in packs.

"Erasmus, did you have something to do with this?" She'd heard of humans pitting animals against each other in blood sports, like cockfighting or lions against bears—there was no contest there. Bears always won. But skunks versus woodpeckers? It was just her luck that the skunks had a human ally. The odds weren't going to be equal at all. Callie would just have to sort that out later.

She watched open-mouthed as the skunks climbed the trees and began to claw out the insects they needed to survive, undoubtedly endangering some woodpecker nests along the way. But looking up high among the branches, she saw it wasn't just woodpeckers she saw but several skunks. The logging was pushing them together, and they were competing for the same place to live.

A dozen woodpeckers attacked the brigade of skunks, defending their nests. A furious battle ensued, until the ground was littered with dead peckers.

Maybe she could intervene and at least bring the carnage to a halt. But she also knew that even one skunk could be formidable. She needed help. Cal whistled softly. A cloud of silver fur stepped out of the trees. *Sina.*

"You skunks!" Callie yelled. "This here's woodpecker land."

At Erasmus's call, a lone male skunk jumped down from the trees and began stamping his feet at her and Sina.

"Uh, oh," Callie said.

We warned you, Mountain Ma'am. He twisted into a U-shape, so that both his head and rear faced her. He let loose a thick fog of foul-smelling spray from his anal glands, scoring a bullseye on Sina.

Cal fired a shot into the air. "Get 'em out of here, Erasmus, before I have to take measures. You got no business messin' with the order of things in these woods."

46

"And you do?" he asked shrewdly. "These peckers were damaging the trees, makin' them unfit for lumber." Callie swung her gun in his direction. "All right, all right, I was just tryin' to help," he said, leading his charges away. In a twinkling, Erasmus and his skunks faded into the forest.

"Some help," Callie snorted to Erasmus's retreating back.

Callie and Sina withdrew to town to reconsider their ill-fated interference. Sina was in a bad way and could barely breathe, tears gushing out of her golden eyes, and Cal could hardly stand to be near her. This was going to require a tomato juice bath. Unfortunately the only tomatoes in town were in her garden. It was a crying shame to use them all up on a wolf-dog instead of the feast she was expecting, but Sina was grateful.

If Cal could get the battling to end, the skunks would probably go to their dens to hibernate for the winter, and the peckers would migrate south. A solution would require bringing it to the attention of the townfolk—who had unknowingly brought it about in the first place. That caused her to perspire not a little. Erasmus worked for Dexter, and reasoning with Dexter's hard-headed loggers would be a challenge.

The logging was already done. Maybe if the road was re-routed. . . But who'd do that for some pesky woodpeckers?

She headed over to the makeshift temporary church, where Father Dyer was preaching a sermon before setting off to the next town. A big crowd had gathered to get churched. Cal tossed some money into the hat going around, and saw the Father smile at her.

"Let us all sing, 'Blest Be the Tie That Binds,'" Father Dyer said.

After the services, Callie asked him if he'd come to lunch over at the Lucky Lady, her treat. That was the start of a long friendship. Callie told him about what she'd seen in the forest.

"Man is the steward of the animals on earth," Father Dyer intoned at his next sermon. "The logging down south is hurting the wildlife," he added, outdoing himself. The ladies in the congregation were all too happy to do God's work by raising the alarm, and they pressured Dexter into agreeing to temporarily divert the road until fall set in.

Callie and Sina cautiously approached the ridge to give the animals the news. They invited Erasmus along as a precaution.

"There's room for everybody now," Callie argued persuasively. "No use wiping each other out, ain't that right, Erasmus?"

A low growl from Sina sealed the deal, and truce was declared.

Cal sighed. Humans might not even miss the two nuisances, but what did they know?

***

As yellow aspen leaves tumbled down the street, Cal stood on the porch showing the ropes to Manuelita, the new housekeeper for the Lucky Lady. She swept a last pile of dirt into the dustpan and handed over the broom and pan.

She contemplated the strange animal feud that had broken out around Leadville and knew it was her work to help keep the balance. She would try to ensure that skunks and woodpeckers were protected in Colorado, pitiful creatures as they were. She was the Mountain Ma'am, after all.

A flock of about 30 woodpeckers crossed the intense blue sky overhead, journeying on the north wind to their winter lands. It was going to be easier to protect the woodpeckers. They were migratory, and not very good eating.

Callie smiled. After taking a lot of joshing in town for the way he stank, Erasmus had said he was moving to California.

Time to get back to bartending.

She noticed a good-looking feller in a shearling jacket coming her way down Harrison Street. She untied her apron and tucked a wisp of red hair behind her ear.

"Drink, mister?" she called.

***

His name was Johnny, and he came from Pennsylvania. He was going to set up a general store and settle in Leadville. He came over for dinner at the saloon every night, and the girls buzzed around him like flies. She had to shoo them all away, because Johnny and she were already nearly a couple, after all. They'd even gone skinny-dipping together last night after the saloon closed.

But Callie wasn't going to make the same mistake she did with her first husband. She promised herself she'd take it slow. Besides, Johnny probably wouldn't understand when she explained about her being the Mountain Ma'am, and all.

"I know all about it, Red," Johnny said, pulling out a locket with her picture in it.

Finally, some of that help Cal had been wanting.

*****～～～～～*****

Whalebone Corset

I had finally found a home in Leadville, Colorado, back in 1883. The beautiful Kitty Furtado had been the first to spot me when I had stumbled down out of the mountains, half-starved and wearing a grizzly bear coat. I carried a Sharps rifle, and a wolf followed close at my heels.

Kitty stepped up to me and said, "Oh you pore thing," and grabbed me by the arm. She glanced at the wolf, which vanished up the street and into the hills.

"I s'pose someone told you I'd be coming, right?" I said, only half-joking.

You see, I'd met Kitty before. In fact, I spent several years as a child sweeping up at the Teller House in Central City. Kitty was the singer there, and she managed the place. But, it was quite a coincidence to see her here in Leadville.

"Well, now, I think Sina told you we were expecting you—as well as who you really are," Kitty said.

My heart began to pound. I had just survived near two months of hardship in the high-country, freezing, starving, and hearing strange things like I was a madwoman. Here Kitty was telling me that what I seen and heard was real. It just couldn't be. Could it?

"Tewa the bobcat is my lookout," Kitty said. "She spotted you, and that's when I notified Sina about your whereabouts."

"Sina." The she-wolf that had come into town with me. A real brave wolf. If anyone had seen her on the street, they would have gone in and got their rifles and shot her on sight. Nowadays there are hardly any wolves left. I was afraid to even think about having a wolf as a friend, but Kitty refreshed my memory.

"Sina is head of the Sawatch Range Tribe, and you are head of the Appalachian Tribe. You know that now. You are the Mountain Ma'am. . ."

". . . and you are head of the Front Range of the Laramide Nation," I finished. This was too incredible. Talking animals and mountain ranges and tribes.

But the experiences I'd had in the mountains had purified me like fire, readying me and convincing me that I needed to come down to civilization to help work things out between Nature and humans.

Kitty got me cleaned up and staked me enough to lease a boarding house in Leadville. I named it the Lucky Lady, added a saloon, and moved in upstairs. Kitty also gave me the news that I was a free woman. My spoiled husband, Harry, who I'd run away from, had gotten himself shot dead after cheating at a Faro game at the Teller. I always wondered if Kitty had dealt him an extra card, but like I've said before, there are some questions better left unasked.

Right about then I started having the dreams. I was running through the hills in the moonlight, the cool air blowing through my hair. I dreamed that big wolf Sina was with me, though I hadn't seen her since I came to Leadville. Our footsteps were light, and we nearly flew. Then all of a sudden the ground gave out below me, and I was tumbling down a cliff. As I hit the bottom, a big wall of flames sprang up, causing me to throw up my hands against my face. I always woke up then, sobbing and scared to death.

As Kitty prepared to return to Central City, I grasped her hand tightly, sorry to see my only human friend leave. She gently pried my fingers loose and said, "You'll be fine. I know it looks like it's going to be near impossible standing against the hordes of greedy people who are coming out West, but I know you can do it. The mountains and the tribes are depending on you. And more help is on the way."

I wasn't so sure I was up to it, but I thanked her and waved her out of town, tears streaming down my smile as she rode away. Kitty was right about how hard my work would become—and how hard it continues to be.

So, at age 16, I threw myself into running the boarding house. There were plenty of customers, mostly working men. Like locusts, over 30,000 folks overran Leadville in just a decade or two. Silver and lead ore shipped out on the narrow gauge around the clock. Between hours of making up beds, washing sheets, and polishing marble washbasins, I played banjo in the saloon and sang my favorite tune, "Liza Jane."

The visions and nightmares continued on and off for a few months, and in some I heard the howls of a wolf and the screams of a big cat echoing off the hills. It was getting so's I couldn't sleep at night, so I began going out on the wood porch and contemplatin' the night sky.

***

As summer came around again, I began to roam around the nearby hills, like I had back when I was running away from Harry.

It was glorious seeing Nature at night. There ain't nothing prettier than a field of blue flax by the light of the full Strawberry Moon. The sounds and sights were beautiful, although at first I didn't know what all I was hearing and seeing. I would come back to town by morning and do the chores before heading to the new town library to find out what I could from books. I was happy that a Scottish gentleman had sent money to our town to build a library, and spent many a happy hour there studying.

I became real strong and fast in those early years. I could cover more and more ground in my wanderings.

Then one night I headed up toward Turquoise Lake and heard a voice in my head:

Mountain Ma'am.

I looked and saw gold-reflecting eyes staring back at me. The she-wolf, Sina.

"I ain't seen you for a while," I said, going right up to her. I never had that much sense.

A tribe leader is coming.

"You mean Kitty?" I asked.

No, he is from the eastern mountains.

He? That was intriguing. Young? Old? But Sina didn't seem to care much about human appearances, so I could only imagine. She and I spent a companionable night exploring the hills, until the lightening sky meant I had to go on home. I felt excited that the help Kitty had promised was on the way. Maybe he could tell me what the dreams meant.

***

Sure enough, a few weeks later as I was sweeping off the porch of the Lucky Lady, I saw a good-looking feller in a shearling jacket coming my way down Harrison Street. His name was Johnny, and he hailed from Pennsylvania, in the Blue Ridge Mountains. In fact, he was the tribe leader.

I offered him a drink, and asked him why he had come out West.

"The Laramide Council all agreed you could use a hand here," was all he said, with a twinkle in his eye. I certainly agreed, and in no time we mated for life. Johnny opened up a general store, and we lived together above the Lucky Lady. Though Johnny was a civilized fellow, he said that, like me, he often felt the call of the wild at night, and we would go patrolling together. Sina would occasionally appear and accompany us, her white teeth flashing as she loped alongside us.

At first those years were uneventful, and the people who flooded into Leadville co-existed peacefully with most of the wildlife around, with the notable exception of wolves.

Then, around '88, I was taken aback to see an older gentleman I once knew come into town and take a seat in my saloon. He sported a gold lion head cane and an old-fashioned beaver top hat.

"Hello, Callie," he said.

I was stunned that he remembered me. It was my first husband's father. It looked like the famous mining mogul, Zachariah Lock, had tracked me down.

"I see you've become quite the businesswoman," he ventured.

I could hardly stand to look at his smarmy face. He had given me no end of grief when I'd lured away his precious Harry. And while just a teenage snippet too. Well, that was water under the bridge as far as I was concerned. Harry and me were hot and heavy for a little while, and then he drank himself into a corner.

"I just wanted to let you know that Lock Mining is opening up a new plant in Leadville," he said.

"Is that so?" I replied. I wasn't as free as I thought. I began to despair of ever getting away from Harry's people. "I hope that Leadville suits you."

"I'm sure it will," he said. "I've bought all the land south of town and am going to set up a smelting facility."

I bit my lip and tasted blood. A big factory belching smoke into the air, and a bunch of smelting poisons being poured into the Arkansas River. . .

"Well, it's your land," I said, forcing myself to be civil.

"Yes, indeed." Eventually the old buzzard left, and I went running over to the general store to talk to Johnny.

"We'll just have to keep an eye out," Johnny said, all level-headed. "We've got a lot of friends here, so if he tries to pull a fast one or hurt us, we'll be all right."

A' course, Johnny didn't know about the Locks. They had moved out here after the Civil War to make their fortune, and they didn't let anybody stand in their way.

***

My life's always been a melodrama, but not usually the kind they do at the theater. Some of Leadville's richest citizens frequented the Lucky Lady, and Leadville was developing some High Society. We were welcomed in, much to my surprise. Horace Tabor's new wife Baby Doe took me under her wing, like a big sister. They built a fancy new opera house with their silver money, and invited me to see a show.

It was a real deluxe place, though, and I had nothing to wear. Baby Doe sent me down to the corsetier, and I got myself fitted for a real whalebone corset with busks at the front and laces up the back. Though it wasn't easy to breathe in, it did sit me up straight as a statue. I thought the black and green dress I bought made me look like a princess, although I was a freckly, red-haired one.

The night before my first opera, I was trying on my new clothes, when I caught a cadaverous reflection in the diamond dust mirror. I twirled around and looked out the window, but there was nothing there. I could have sworn it was that evil old man Lock. Maybe I had gotten overly sensitive lately, I thought. I shrugged it off and tried to put it out of my mind.

A little while after Lock came to town, Johnny and I walked back from a performance of Wagner's "Siegfried" opera. We'd had a real fine time.

"I loved that story, didn't you?" I said. "Especially the part about those Valkyrie warrior women flying around through the air, and that little bird telling Siegfried to steal the ring and helmet."

"Yes, it reminded me a little of you, Mountain Ma'am," Johnny said. "But Brunhilde's father putting her inside a wall of fire was a little cruel, though."

I didn't mention that I'd started having a lot more dreams about fire lately.

***

The saloon was doing a booming business, what with the new miners and factory workers pouring in to work at the Lock smelter. But the original settlers began to notice the air begin to smell like burning tar. The mayor got a lot of complaints but seemed powerless to do anything about it. Anyone who crossed Lock seemed to have bad luck, like the newspaper reporter on the Leadville Chronicle who got crushed in the printing press. Folks said she was sleepwalking.

We had a wayfaring preacher called Father Dyer, who traveled around from town to town preaching the gospel and helping bring some civility to the mostly wild men that lived out West in those days. In the winter, when the passes were closed to horses and trains, Father Dyer would strap on the skis he made out of barrel slats and travel to give his next sermon. One summer's day he hiked in and stopped by the Lucky Lady to see if he could get a donation to a church he wanted to build in Breckenridge.

Me and Johnny were happy to put money in the hat, but we weren't Christians by any means, not since we had learned that the earth's history for the past several thousand years had been a whole lot different from what the Bible said. Still, we liked the messages in the Bible about stewarding the land and the animals and offered him our hospitality.

"Come on in, Father," I said to the old man. "You set right down here. We got some great venison stew on the cook stove that you might like. Some real tasty carrots right out of my back garden, too."

Father Dyer and I got into some lively conversations about the origins of the world.

"We are all part of God's Creation," he kept saying, when I said the mountains were ancient, and the animals and Indians hereabouts had been here long before the easterners got here. Johnny wisely stayed out of it. The preacher had his old-time religion, and I had my old religion. Father Dyer ate his fill and said he was setting out to visit the folks over in Twin Lakes.

"It's probably different from what you remember, Father," I said. "Big new smelting plant's gone in since you was last here."

The Father thanked us and headed out the door. Me and Johnny shot each other that "he's gonna get a surprise" look.

A week later, Father Dyer was back.

"Well, hello, Father. What brings you back so soon?"

"A whole lot of death," he said. "It was terrible."

"Why? What's happened?" I asked. I hadn't gotten any news about a disaster. That was more the sort of thing that attracted preachers and morticians.

"He's been locking his workers in and working them until they get sick. Then they disappear. I was ministering to a few of the sick ones, and they was begging me to get them out before he came after them."

"He? You mean Lock?"

"Yes—and his men. I was lucky to get out myself. When I hiked out, I saw a lot of fresh graves hidden behind the smelter. He's digging another big hole out there too. We've got to warn people."

"We'll tell folks, Father. Thanks for letting us know."

That night Johnny and I decided to take a little stroll down south to Twin Lakes instead of our more usual saunter over to Turquoise.

58

Tossing my clothes on a chair, I pulled on some dungarees and one of Johnny's work shirts, tucking my .44 into my belt. I pulled my Sharps off the mantle, and slipped out the back with Johnny.

Sina, I called. I hoped she would show up. We needed her night vision. And her nose. With our little noses, all we would smell would be burning coal and melted ore.

We walked about two miles to the south, where we could hear the clanging machinery of the smelter. I judged we were a little to the north of the smelter and went off to the right so we could see what was behind the plant.

A brush of fur against my fingers told me that Sina had joined us. In the darkness, she looked like a pale gray ghost.

We walked quietly to the area Father Dyer had described. We heard a couple of men talking. They had what looked like bundles of trash, and they were digging.

"That's probably good enough for now," one said. "Get the oil of vitriol. And be careful. That stuff dissolves everything!"

In my haste to get a closer look, I stumbled over a root and fell headlong.

"Who's there?" the man shouted. He quickly found me and leveled his pistol at my head.

"It's a woman," he said, sounding surprised. "Well, you've come to the wrong place, gal. You're just going to have to join these other folks here."

What other folks? Now I knew what the bundles were.

"Please, mister—" I started to say, but then one of them hit me across the back of the head, and I was falling into the big hole.

"No time for the vitriol now," I heard him say. He grabbed a can of kerosene and poured it over the bundles, pushing each into the hole. He pulled out his matches and lit one, holding it high in the air. I watched as he flicked it over into the hole where I was pinned by the weight of who-knows-who.

Two rapid-fire arrows pierced the men's chests, and they keeled over. Then Johnny was peering over the edge, calling for me. I was coughing and yelling, and Sina was barking. Johnny climbed down and pushed me up just before the whole thing went up in a wall of flame. Sina pulled me back from the searing heat.

I was afraid we'd lost Johnny. But there he was, his sheepskin jacket singed but none the worse for wear. We heard some voices, as someone from town noticed the fire and started a clangor. Sina turned, saying *"Farewell, Mountain Ma'am,"* before disappearing in that uncanny way she had. Sina seemed burned pretty badly by the kerosene and vitriol and needed time to lick her wounds.

We limped away, heading back to town. We didn't wait until morning before we went to the sheriff's.

The sheriff led a posse to Twin Lakes, where they found twenty workers locked in a shed. Like Father Dyer had said, some were sick, and they'd been kept from leaving. At least they were still alive.

When folks heard about the imprisoned workers and the murders, they shut the smelter down. Lock left town and escaped arrest. That's one of my big regrets. But I'm sure if Father Dyer is right, Lock'll get his just deserts for all the harm he's done, either here or wherever he's going.

***

After the smelter closed, Johnny and I thought all our worries were over. We celebrated by taking in another of Baby Doe's operas.

"I need to drop by the store to check on some deliveries. Why don't you go on ahead and meet me back home at the boarding house," Johnny said. "Did I mention you looked real purty tonight?"

"I bet you say that to all the gals," I said.

"Only the ones who've got their bubbies uplifted," he said, snapping the top of my corset. "Wait up for me, and I'll be right back." I turned a corner and headed down the alley behind Harrison Street, prepared to go up the wooden staircase out back of the hotel leading to our bedroom.

Someone must have been watching us for a long time. We always did our nocturnal ramblings out the back door, and this person knew that. I lifted up my skirt and placed a foot on the first stair, when a noose tightened around my neck and lifted me off the ground. I kind of panicked at first, and I couldn't breathe. Little flashes of darkness were gathering across my eyes as I clawed at my neck.

Then my fingertips brushed against the ridges of my corset. I pulled open the loosely bow-tied bodice of my dress and grabbed the front edge, ripping the busks away. I kicked backward and got him to set me down a minute, then crouched down and sprang up into his chin. My hard head threw him back a bit, and let me turn around and pluck a stay out of my corset.

Now I had a razor-sharp piercin' dagger in my hand. I drove it up below his ribs, and he collapsed with an agonized grunt, blood leaking out around his hand where he tried to hold it in.

Just then, Johnny and Sina showed up, and Johnny let out with a kick while Sina tore at the varmint's throat. I fell against the wall, trying to catch my breath.

I must have looked a sight, because Johnny said, "Well, you must be pretty anxious to see me, my purty little ma'am, takin' off your clothes already."

"You better be joking, Johnny Wellborn," I croaked, my voice hoarse from the near choking I'd taken.

Johnny swooshed me up, took me upstairs, and tossed me on the bed. But then he strode to the door, yanked it open and went outside. He locked it from the outside, and stomped back downstairs. I was in bed when

Johnny stole back into the dark black room. He climbed in beside me, and we lay like spoons until sleep finally came.

I never knew what happened to that man, so I guess Johnny and Sina made sure he disappeared. It was clear someone was still out to get me, and I figured it was Lock. My whalebone corset always was missing a stay after that. I began carrying it along with my .44 and my Sharps whenever we'd go out prowling.

Until Sina showed up and helped Johnny take care of that murderin' cutthroat, I'd been a little unsure of my ability to reach out to her. Now I knew we were to have many more adventures together. How did I know? A little birdie told me.

I hope Sina didn't eat her.

*****~~~~~*****

Doc Frain

A high-pitched voice cut through Callie Wellborn's reverie.

"Didn't get enough sleep last night?" Mrs. Schott from the Walker Ranch was coming down the street, headed her way.

"What? Oh, I guess not," Callie replied, and made a couple of feeble sweeping motions with her broom.

In truth Callie had been daydreaming about last week's show at the new Leadville Opera House. A troupe from Denver had presented Shakespeare's "A Midsummer Night's Dream," and she couldn't get the spectacle of kings and fairies out of her mind. A' course, she'd been up most of the night running around the hills, so it wasn't just that.

"What can I do for you, Mrs. Schott? Did you want something from the general store? I think Johnny's due back soon." Johnny's store was about a block down Harrison Street from the Lucky Lady Saloon, and it was getting close to closing time.

"No, thank you dear. I just wanted to know if you'd heard there's a new doctor in town."

"Really? That's real good news, Mrs. Schott. This town could use another pair of medical hands. Old Doc Cowgill is up to his top button in baby deliveries alone, what with Leadville growing by leaps and bounds."

"Yes, but I heerd he's as black as coal," Mrs. Schott continued. "He'll just be tendin' to the coloreds."

Callie was surprised; she figured there were only a few hundred negroes in Colorado Territory. A few worked at the Lock Mining Company smelter, and she bet none of those folks had ever seen a doctor, colored or not. Of course, neither had any of the white people who worked for Lock.

"Yep, he just appeared all of a sudden. Didn't have a horse that anyone could tell, and there weren't no passengers on the narrow gauge in the last week, due to all the cars bein' used by Lock."

"Maybe he hitched a ride with the engineer," Callie suggested. She bit her lip; she'd been tricked into gossiping yet again by Mrs. Schott. She'd promised herself she would stop speculatin' about everyone and everything that came into town. If anything big was up, Sina'd let her know.

"Well, I got to get back to setting up dinner," Callie said. "Thanks for stoppin' by." She turned her back and hastily swept her way through the saloon doors.

Maybe she'd have a dinner theme about midsummer night on the menu. Summer was finally hitting Summit County now that it was nearly July. She changed her mind immediately. These guys were meat and potatoes, not dainty slippers and flowery talk. Still, it would have been nice. . . She started chopping carrots and potatoes for a stew. Even with Manuelita the housekeeper, Callie worked seven-day weeks.

***

Johnny came in after closing up the general store and immediately headed for the dining room, where he sat at the main table filling sugar bowls. Most of them were empty. Them miners sure could go through the sugar. Seemed like their coffee and chickory was half sugar. He didn't look up when the dining room door leading off from the saloon squeaked open.

"We ain't open yet."

"Hello, Mr. Wellborn. I wonder if I might persuade you to open the general store again. I'm sorry I lost track of the time sewing up an injured miner, but I'm fresh out of supplies. I'm the new doctor, Hamand Frain."

"I guess I could do that, Doc." Johnny looked up— and nearly dropped a sugar bowl. A tall, thin black man dressed in knee coat and holding a beaver top hat stood looking down at him. He wore patent shoes, a green damask vest, and a silk puff tie. His hair was startlingly white, and Johnny'd never seen anyone so dressed up in the daytime, except maybe Old Man Lock.

"Thank you, sir. I'd be happy to make it worth your while. I've got some patients to see tomorrow, and I need some grain alcohol to make them up an herbal tonic. Oh, and some sugar to make it palatable."

That figured. Everybody always wantin' more sugar. What was wrong with good old molasses? Johnny stood up and put his hat on as they went outside. It had been warm earlier, but now Johnny noticed a chill breeze blowing. Probably some rain headed their way.

"Jist a sec, let me get my coat," Johnny replied.
***
"Now, where did Johnny go?" Callie said, entering the dining room a minute later. "He didn't put out all the table sugar. Men. They ain't cut out to be housekeepers, that's sure."

That night after 2 o'clock closing, she and Johnny crept out the side stairway from their rooms above the Lucky Lady to do nightly rounds. The hillsides were slippery after the evening's rain, but the two slowly worked their way upward. Sina materialized after they got a few hundred feet above town, the big she-wolf nearly invisible, except for her reflective eyes.

Mountain Ma'am, Sina greeted her. Callie still couldn't get used to the idea that she could hear what the big wolf was thinking. Or that a wolf was the leader of a tribe of creatures in the nearby Sawatch Range. Since she'd met Sina, they'd formed a loose coalition of humans and animals dedicated to preserving these mountains. They called themselves the Uplifted. The night was silent.

"Seen any fairies, Sina?" Callie joked. Johnny looked askance at her.

There is a visitor from the old ranges.

"Really? I was just joshin'," Callie said. "Who is it?"

The Dark One, Hammon.

"The dark one?"

"You don't mean the new doctor, do you?" Johnny cut in. "He's black, you know."

"You've met him?" Callie asked.

"Yes, I helped him at the general store."

Do not aid the Dark One.

"Sina!" Callie said, sounding a little scandalized. Racial feelings were still raw after the War.

He has crossed, although the bridge is gone.

"What bridge?"

"Never mind," Johnny said, taking her arm. "It's getting close to dawn. We've got to run."

***

Callie sat on the bed counting last night's dinner receipts. It was just like Sina to be so cryptic. What did she mean about Doc Frain crossing when there was no bridge? When she finished up here, she would go over to the library and see if there was any folklore about bridges. There weren't any trolls these days, as far as she knew. But if Sina was upset, something was definitely awry.

"Dang, I forgot I said I'd go to the schoolhouse this morning to talk about getting along in the mountains," Callie said. Before finding herself in Leadville, she'd spent the better part of two months in the snowbound high country on her own. That was when she met Sina and the other animals of the Uplifted.

"I was probably delirious from starvation most of the time," she mumbled, "but we won't talk about that part." Since then she'd learned a lot more about living rough from books and, of course, from Johnny. She stuffed the receipts in the lock box and stowed it in the bottom drawer of her dresser. She went to her closet to look for the outfit that would impress the kids no end. The grizzly bear rug she'd worn as a coat, tied shut with a leather string. The string came in handy for catching rabbits, so she'd show how to make a snare.

She decided against taking the Sharps rifle hanging above the mantlepiece in the bar or her .44 pistol. That was for the kids' parents to teach them.

Heading over to the schoolhouse, she greeted Miss O'Malley, the teacher. Emmaline O'Malley wasn't much older than Callie, but she'd been put in charge of a pack of howling schoolchildren and rose admirably to the task.

"Quiet, children," she shouted, and the hubbub gradually died down. "Today we're in for a treat. As you all know, Mrs. Callie Wellborn from the Lucky Lady is going to show us how to survive in the wilderness. First, I'll call the roll."

It looked like everyone was present, except for one boy, Davey.

"He was so looking forward to this, Mrs. Wellborn," Emmaline called Callie by her formal name. "He was so disappointed when he came down sick."

Callie did her little show and tell, and was rewarded by clapping, whistling, and cheering, especially from the boys. The girls were a little quieter, unable to imagine a lady cutting up a big elk and evicting wild animals from a cave so she could cook it. Emmaline excused the students for recess and thanked Callie for coming.

"Would it help if I dropped by to see Davey?" Callie offered.

"Oh, would you? I'm sure he'll have something to brag about to the others if you make a special visit."

"I'd be happy to," Callie said, gathering up her grizzly coat and other props. Davey's house was only a block away, and she could swing by the Library after that.

She knocked on the door. Davey's mother answered the door and seemed surprised to see Callie. She looked over her shoulder and hesitated to invite Callie in.

"I jist dropped by to say hello to Davey. Heard he was sick and missed the show at school."

"Er, yes," his mother said. "It's just that the doctor is here seeing him now."

"Oh, then I'll just come some other—" Callie started to say.

"I gave him something to make him sleep," a deep voice said from the back room. A tall man stepped out into the parlor, wiping his hands on a towel. Davey's mother looked embarrassed.

"Davey was so sick, and Dr. Frain kindly offered to take a look at him."

The man was undoubtedly dark-skinned, but he was not like any negro Callie had ever seen. Callie decided it couldn't hurt to welcome the new doc.

"Pleased to meet you," she said, reaching out her hand. "I'm Callie Wellborn." The doctor smiled widely, and shook it.

It was a strange, not unwelcome sensation, as he wrapped his long fingers around her wrist and hand. The doctor's handshake made her feel warm, and her heart skipped a beat. He held her hand a little too long, and then released it. Callie swayed a little and caught herself. He grinned. "Now, see you don't come down with the same thing," he said.

"Here is a tonic for the young lad," he said, turning to Davey's mother. "Give him a tablespoon every three hours. I'll check back on him tomorrow."

"I'm sure that won't be necessary, Doctor," she replied. Callie could tell she was already worried about gossips in town.

"Good day, ladies," Doc Frain said, putting his hat on and stepping out the front door.

The women stared at each other. "Davey met the doc last week when he first came to town. When he got sick, he kept asking for Dr. Frain. He's been getting dreadful pale, so I did what he asked, pore thing."

"I'm sure you did the right thing calling the Doc," Callie said. "Listen, I've got to be going, but I'm glad to see Davey's going to get well." Time to get down to the library.

Callie said hello to the librarian and went straight back to the bookshelf she needed. The shelf was always dusty, as if no one ever looked at these books. She'd tried dusting before, but the shelf always looked neglected.

Sometimes she had to look for days to find a clue about what Sina meant. She wondered how this knowledge got passed down to the Laramide Nation leaders. They sure as hell didn't read, and they weren't very talkative. Except when they felt like it.

She picked a book on mountain history and turned to the contents.

No, there didn't seem to be any chapters about dark ones. There was a chapter about the history of mountain peoples and tribes, though. She sat down at a table and began leafing through it. She was surprised to learn that there used to be a bridge of land from the other side of the ocean, and how the First People and animals came over that land to what was now America. They settled in the mountain ranges, including the Appalachians and the Laramides. But that was thousands of years ago.

She sighed and pulled out another volume, titled, "Mysteries of Folklore." The frontispiece had the slogan, "Respect the realm of mysteries." Aha, here was something on myths about alternate worlds, including Kyrnwood, Land of the Fairies. She smiled, recalling the Shakespeare play the other night. Wouldn't it be funny if Doc Frain was a fairy? He was a little big to be riding a hummingbird, though. She laughed out loud. The librarian directed a warning frown in her direction.

Well, Doc probably wasn't one of the Fae, anyway. They were an amoral race who preyed upon humans, stealing their babies. The old myths said time in Kyrnwood passed much more slowly than here, so that once you went there you had to stay. If you came back, you'd suddenly grow old and die. Despite his white hair, Doc was quite young, and would do a lot of good helping folks get well.

***

But Davey didn't get well; he got worse. Callie took over some corn muffins—about the only thing she could cook worth a darn, 'cept for rabbit stew—and found Doc Frain ministering to the boy.

Davey's skin had taken on a deathly pallor, the kind of grayish blue that Callie had seen too often. Her worried look must have caught Doc's eye, because he put his hand on her shoulder to comfort her. He really was a wonderful doctor, she thought, feeling hopeful again. She left off her basket and shook the doctor's hand before stepping out on the porch. She could still feel the tingle in her hand as she stood daydreaming, until a deafening barrage of noise from a woodpecker against the railing shook her awake. She recovered herself and began walking back toward the Lucky Lady.

She had gotten about fifty yards up the street, when she heard Doc's kindly voice.

"Callie, there's no need to worry, now, you hear, girl?"

"Yes, Doc," she said. He took a step closer to touch her face. A sudden growl stopped him in his tracks. It was Sina, there in broad daylight.

"Sina, git, you hear?" Callie hissed. If anyone saw the she-wolf, she'd get shot for sure.

Be gone, Enchanter.

Doc only laughed. "I see you got a pet dog, Callie. Shoo, you cur, or I'll skin you and hang you out to dry. She's mine now."

Callie should have been shocked by this threat to Sina, but instead she just stood there, transfixed by his beautiful voice. It was beautiful, but it made her feel sad at the same time.

"Well, good day to you, Mrs. Wellborn. I'll be seeing you soon." Doc tipped his hat. Sina was nowhere in sight.

***

After a day of visiting the sick, Callie wasn't feeling all that well herself. That night when it was time to make the rounds with Johnny, she begged off. She'd fought strange creatures in her nightmares all last night, and she felt drained.

"That's too bad," Johnny said. "I ain't never seen you sick a day. I'll see you at dawn, then, sweetie," he said, and slipped into his buckskin jacket. It got pretty cold outside at night, even in the summer. Callie didn't reply and sat listlessly on the bed.

Johnny met up with Sina and told her the Mountain Ma'am was feeling poorly.

She belongs to the Dark One.

Well, didn't that beat all. Callie was lying to him so's she could sneak out and see that Doc Frain. Johnny was both hurt and jealous. He ran extra hard that night to get the anger out of his system, dealing harsh treatment to miscreants who had the misfortune to get in his path. Tomorrow he'd confront the man. Frain wasn't gonna steal his Callie away from him, not after all Johnny went through to make her his. Sina too was angry; she had tried to protect the humans, but the Dark One had tricked her by taking the child instead of a baby. Johnny dragged himself in to the bedroom before dawn, totally exhausted. Callie was sitting in the exact same place she was when he

71

left, still dressed. Johnny felt fury rise in his throat. They weren't gonna make a fool out of *him*.

***

Callie kept saying she was too tired or too sick to patrol at night, until Johnny started to feel maybe she was telling the truth. But Sina never lied. He wrote two notes, one for Kitty and one for Callie's fathers, Frank and Jesse, over in Central City. It looked like Callie was wasting away from love, and it might be good if they could come. A few days later, the three arrived after a grueling series of narrow gauge train rides on the Colorado Central Railroad, the Colorado and Southern, and finally the High Line up to Leadville. Johnny offered them rooms in the boardinghouse next to the Lucky Lady.

Kitty untied her feathered boa. She hadn't even changed out of her dancehall costume before coming. They went upstairs to Johnny and Callie's bedroom overlooking the street.

Kitty yelled at Johnny when she saw how ill Callie had become. It was like all the Mountain Ma'am's vibrant energy had drained away.

"Ain't you been feeding her?"

"She always says she isn't hungry," Johnny replied. He realized that wasn't like Callie at all and vowed to fry her up a skillet of her favorite bacon. The smell alone should tempt her.

Johnny pointed out the window at the man standing on the boardwalk opposite. Doc Frain had brazenly taken up a post across the street, staring up toward their bedroom and smoking cigarillo after cigarillo. Kitty pulled down the shade.

"That man's got some power over her. It's all she can do to resist," Kitty scolded. "Look at her."

Frank and Jesse weren't so sure that was the story. This wouldn't be the first time Callie became infatuated with some no-good scoundrel.

"Look at when she ran off at fourteen and married Harry Lock. She doesn't have the sense God gave a turnip about picking men," Frank said. Johnny scowled. "Present company excepted," Frank amended.

"What has she been doing lately, besides sitting here in her room?" Kitty asked.

"She kept visiting a sick little boy from school," Johnny said. "That's where she met Doc Frain. Oh, and she went to the library to look up some Dark One that Sina was going on about. I thought it was a bunch of nonsense because Doc is a negro."

"The Dark One? The king of the fairies? Why didn't you say so in the first place?" Kitty said in an exasperated tone.

"Yes, that's what he is, a king," Callie said. "He came across a bridge—no, a portal—from Faerie, and he's taking me back with him. It's just like a midsummer night's dream."

"I'm surrounded by fools," Kitty retorted. That man's a menace to Mountain Ma'am, and through her, to everyone on earth. We thought we had his folk bottled up in the old world—they can't get across the water. But he's found his way to our plane somehow. It happened once before, but old Ben Franklin smashed their portal with a bolt of lightning. We've been enemies since before anyone can remember." She thought a moment, then turned toward Johnny.

"I'm pretty sure I know how he got here. Johnny, for once, all those muscles of yours are going to come in handy for something besides attracting pretty girls. Here's what we're going to do. . ."

***

Johnny tightened the rope around his waist and tugged experimentally on it. It would be a thousand foot drop if it broke.

Kitty, Johnny, Frank, Jesse, and Sina had spent half the night planning this heist. Johnny had handled dynamite before, and he even stocked it for the miners at the store, but actually using it was another matter. Frank and Jesse agreed to handle that end, if Johnny and Sina could just do the acrobatics.

They rehearsed the plan over and over, until finally Kitty said, "Today's Sunday. Let's do it."

Johnny went upstairs to get Callie. She sat with a look of intense concentration, rubbing her wrists a little.

"You all right, darlin'"?

"I just wish these handcuffs was looser," Callie replied, as if sleep-talking to no one in particular. "They are startin' to burn."

Johnny helped her to her feet and led her downstairs, where Kitty waited in the deserted Lucky Lady.

"Give me and Sina half an hour to get to the tunnel," he told Kitty, "then let the fairy have her." He'd said he wasn't happy with using Callie as bait, but the leaders of the Uplifted felt it was the best chance they had. Johnny and Sina vanished up the street.

Kitty held Frank's train watch and counted the minutes. She was alone with Callie now, while the men lay in wait. She took a deep breath and gently pushed Callie out onto the street.

Too quickly for the human eye to detect, Doc Frain swooped by and pulled Callie into the sky. He was gone in an instant, leaving only a faint green trail where he had disturbed the air.

***

Johnny dangled from a rope above the new tunnel bore that now connected both sides of the Continental Divide, when he heard the sound of a train whistle. It was traveling at an unearthly speed, and as it got closer, Johnny could see that the engineer wasn't human. Johnny shouted, "He's here, on the train!" Just like Kitty said.

Johnny released the rope just as the train streaked into the tunnel and landed on top of the car behind the locomotive. A huge explosion rocked the west end, spraying tons of rock onto the track. Crouching aboard the racing train, Johnny could see a glittering maelstrom ahead where daylight should have been—the bridge to Kyrnwood. He spotted Frain and Callie in the third car and felt a bump as Sina leaped onto the roof beside him. They ran to the coupler, jumped down, and burst into the passenger car.

Distracted by the explosion, Frain looked out the window, while Callie sat quietly, gazing at her imaginary handcuffs. With a tremendous roar, Sina pounced and sank her teeth into Frain's throat. Viridian blood sprayed in all directions as she ripped and shook him. The train braked sharply, shooting sparks from the wheels. The Fae engineer opened the door to the car, saw Frain, and did an abrupt about-face, disappearing into the portal.

Callie awoke from her trance. "Johnny? Sina?" She surveyed the ransacked train car.

"We got to go, gal," Johnny replied. "Hurry." They climbed out of the car and ran for the small keyhole that remained near the top of the west end of the tunnel. There was no way the train would be able to back out this direction. They clambered out of the opening, and Johnny yelled, "Blow it!"

A series of detonations caved in the whole bore. When the smoke and dust cleared a little, they could see Frank and Jesse waving at them from the hillside above.
    ***

"I shore am hungry," Callie said, eating her fifth piece of bacon and washing it down with a mug of coffee. "I'd liked to have starved to death if you guys hadn't rescued me." She had slept for two straight days since the Continental Tunnel "disaster." It made the newspapers all the way to Denver.

Kitty smiled and handed Callie a napkin. "I don't think any of the fairies will be back. We bounced the portal back to the plane of dreams, and even if people rebuild the tunnel, it won't work any more as a bridge. But just to be sure, I'll post some of the Uplifted to keep an eye on it."

"I never expected another kind of folk existed," Callie said. "Real devious ones, too. Say, does anyone know if Davey survived?"

"He's a tough little guy," Johnny replied. "Sina and I peeked in on rounds last night, and he's recovering well. I think Frain lost interest in him once he latched on to you. If you hadn't hung on long enough to tell us about the portal, Callie, no telling what Frain could have got up to."

"I aim to serve," Callie said. "Now, pass me over some more of them biscuits," would you?

###

*****~~~~~*****

The Chimera and the Coin

When I was a girl, I felt more comfortable with my best friend Sina—a gray she-wolf— than I did with people. My heart broke when she died of old age, and I was even sadder that almost every wolf in these parts was being wiped out by the miners, ranchers, and anybody with a gun. Didn't they know wolves are a natural part of the life in these mountains? I felt like a failure.

I talked about it with my husband Johnny. He runs the general store here in Leadville.

"It's even worse over on the Front Range," he said. "There haven't been any Colorado wolves spotted in years."

"Ain't there anything we can do?" I asked him.

"Probably not, beyond going to join them in the spirit world," he said softly.

Sina was a wise and wily foe, and avoided most humans. Her huge size made her formidable, and anyone encountering her usually ran the other way. She mostly didn't bother to give chase, unless she was defending me or Johnny. Even when folks got it into their heads to try to eradicate the wolves, she always managed to evade her pursuers. But the one thing she couldn't evade was time. Her once thick silvery coat began to fall out, and her arthritic legs could no longer chase down enough game to feed herself. Johnny and I wanted to keep her alive by hunting deer and rabbits for her, but eventually Sina no longer would even take what was laid in front of her. I leaned close to her as she lay there, panting quietly and in pain.

"Eat, Sina. You're going to get better."

The light left her eyes, and she turned her head away.

"No, Sina! I love you. Please!" But she was already gone. She'd already lived nearly twice as long as the average wild wolf. Johnny wrapped her in a blanket, and we buried her near her den, so she could feel at home.

Do wild animals think about life after death? It's hard to say, and I was acquainted with a lot of animals. They all lived their lives the best they could, and that was it. I thought I'd never see Sina's likes again. Yet I knew that a spirit world existed. I knew so in the same way that I knew that the world of the Laramide Nation around us was real—not jist some fancy, passing and insubstantial. But could anyone visit the dead and come back? I didn't really want to leave Johnny jist yet. He couldn't cook for himself worth a darn. Even so, I wasn't expectin' to go to Hell so soon.

After Sina left us, I didn't have any nightmares or "feelings" about what was to come. In fact, I hadn't had any Mountain Ma'am dreams or premonitions in years. Jist like I hadn't heard from any wolves in a long time. Was I losing my gift, if you can call it that? That scared me more than some of the old visions. Between Johnny's talk of the spirit world, and nostalgia for the old days, I got more and more restless. I'd walk down the boardwalk, and it seemed like even the horses would turn an accusing eye on me. Sometimes you don't know what you've got until you lose it. Despite Johnny's support, I was feeling a yearning that's hard to explain.

Maybe someone else had older knowledge, knew the ancient myths, and would pow-wow serious-like to a mere snip of a gal like me. I figured that would be one of the First People. We called them Indians back then. The Laramide Nation leaders in America originally were First

People. In the last 300 years or so, Johnny and my folks settled here too. I guess we got recruited because Leadville is at a real high altitude, and most of the Indians lived farther down, although Lake County was the Shoshone's old hunting grounds. And, like the wolves, most of the First People who lived in our range had moved up to Wyoming.

That restless feeling pulled on me until I felt I had to go to Wyoming, to the Wind River Reservation in particular. Sacagawea's grandson lived there, although this wasn't her "white" grandson, Pompy, and he wasn't famous except to us Laramides. He was called Daka.

Johnny said he was worried about me going so far away.

"What do you expect to do, Red?" he asked.

"I don't know for sure. I only know it's got something to do with Sina—with wolves," I said.

"You know Sina's never coming back, don't you, Callie? She's dead and gone."

"I know. I helped to bury her. But I've been reading about how the Shoshones have this myth about being founded by wolves. There's also some myths about the spirit world—tales about going there and talking to dead folks."

"Yeah, I heard those tales too, but. . . Oh, I see it now, you want to talk with them about visiting Sina."

I never could keep a secret from Johnny.

"Not jist visiting her. I want to get her back. And any of her pack that wants to come back with me."

"What would you do if you got a pack of wolves? People'd just shoot them again."

"I don't know. I jist want them back. It ain't right with them gone."

"Well, I'm going with you, you hard-headed woman. But if that Shoshone can't help, we'll come on home, right?"

I agreed to that. Johnny was right. He's right about me being stubborn and hard, but I have to be sensible sometimes. Though we fought it originally, our marriage represented an alliance between two powerful magical mountain tribes.

Johnny hitched up old Rambler, and we set out from Leadville on a beautiful late summer day. Some aspens were already turning, so we would have to make good time if we were to get back before the deep snows. It looked like some artist had painted gold stripes across the dark green, almost black, pines below Vail Pass. A yellow scab on the landscape showed where miners had dumped tailings years ago.

As we traveled up through the North Park basin, rimmed by mountain ranges on all sides: the Medicine Bow, Never Summer, Rabbit Ears, and Park, we felt our particular gods were watching us. We turned west toward Craig and rode alongside huge herds of elk as they grazed hungrily, building strength for the rutting season. We set up camp and enjoyed the Full Corn Moon, remembering the nights we had roamed in the company of Sina, our close friend and leader of the Sawatch Range.

We crossed into Wyoming and continued north to Rawlins, where we got more supplies. I was delighted to find the store had a supply of huckleberries and chokecherries, 'cause I was sick of hard tack. Johnny made fun of my "lovely purple lips" for two days.

Then about halfway between Rawlins and Lander, a rattler got our horse Rambler. I threw a fit, and did a backwards trajectory to see where the snake was. I heard a faint rattle. She was a mama, covering her nest of little ones. I stomped over to the nest, ignoring the danger rattle, and asked her, "Why the hell did you bite my horse?"

She merely flicked her tongue. *You should not go to Daka, Mountain Ma'am.*

Did *everyone* know I was going to visit the shaman and spirit guide?

"All right, I understand you don't want me to go truck with the spirit world, but did you have to go and kill Rambler?"

He was happy to make the sacrifice for you, Mountain Ma'am.

I thought that was a load of bull pucky, but I'd heard it before, and I knew it was true. I let mama rattler live, because I knew it wasn't her fault.

Johnny borrowed my Sharps and did what needed to be done for Rambler. I 'spose I can't cry over every dead critter, according to Johnny, but this was real rough. And I was going to git there, no matter what. We unloaded the wagon and made the rest of the journey carrying packs. A big bolt of lightning shot across the sky from east to west, and cold rain followed us the next 40 miles, soaking us like drowned rats.

Finally we stumbled our way past Lander, Wyoming, to the Wind River Reservation, home of the Shoshone. We stopped at Fort Washakie to warm ourselves by the fire. I pulled off my wet gloves and asked where we might find Daka. His family lived on a small ranch dotted with alamosa trees a few miles from the fort.

Daka was real hospitable, inviting us to come in, dry off, and stay to a meal. He even offered to let us stay in his teepee out back. But after what I sensed the mama rattler was trying to tell me, I wasn't going to jist trust everything he said.

That night after dinner, Daka's wife and children went to bed, and we sat down for a serious talk.

"I know you are the Mountain Ma'am," Daka said. That surprised me, but now that it was out in the open, I started in asking questions.

"Could you tell me about some of the old myths?" I asked. "I've heard you know all the Shoshone tales." I didn't ask him direct about going to the spirit world.

"You probably want to know about how the Laramide Nation came to be," he offered. I eagerly agreed.

He went on for hours about things I already knew, about how there used to be a bridge of land from the other side of the ocean, and how the First People and animals came over that land. I always found it amusing that our pesky woodpeckers were one of them. The people divided into tribes and settled, mostly close to rivers and mountains, and took up stewarding the land. Then the bridge went under water as the glaciers began to melt. Daka talked like it was the most natural thing in the world for animals and humans to live together. The difference from today was that the animals wanted to control their own lives, they weren't the slaves of humans. Some were even tribe leaders, although that gradually had become a human job, since we are hell-bent on being the boss.

"How do you know about me?" I asked. "Can you talk to animals like me and Johnny?"

"No, but I heard about you a long time ago. Your friend Sina was only a wolf, but we knew she could talk with humans if she wanted. She told the alliance the wolves were in trouble, and asked for help. When you grew, Kitty nominated you as the next Mountain Ma'am, and Sina became your wolf guardian. The Shoshone and the Laramide are allies."

I'd been figuring out a sneaky way to ask about wolves, but Daka had brought it up all on his own!

"Is it possible for me to visit Sina in the spirit land? I want to talk with her more about how we can save the wolf in our range."

"You mean you want Sina back."

I said nothing.

"I don't have the knowledge you seek, Mountain Ma'am," Daka replied. "Even if I did, I'm not sure I would help a white woman, after all the crimes your people have committed."

Johnny stood up and loomed over Daka. "Callie didn't do any of those things you're insinuatin'. Come, on, Cal, let's go."

I tugged on Johnny's sleeve to sit him back down.

"I'm sure no one here wants to give offense, Johnny. Please continue, Daka."

"Right. You didn't give me a chance to finish," Daka said. "I was about to say—you can see that I also want the wolves to survive. Perhaps I *can* help you talk to Sina once more, but that is all."

He sat in thought for while and finally spoke. "The attempt is dangerous, and you can't come back from the spirit world without the token of life."

He reached into his shirt and pulled up a string tied to a leather bag that held a big chunk of turquoise.

"This talisman is more valuable than all the gold your people kill for," he said. "The wearer can walk and talk in the spirit world."

Johnny asked, "Can I go also?"

"Only one," Daka replied. "But we can guide her. Let us rest before the journey."

"Well, now that you menfolk have it all figured out," I said sarcastically. "I do believe I'll take my chances. But I'm thankful for the offer of the loan of the talisman, Daka."

The next day we carried a pipe and other supplies away from Daka's ranch, hiking until we came to a bluff with sandstone and rocks jutting out from the sagebrush. The basin below the bluff sloped gradually into a large, shallow crater. A fine mist hovered over the ground, as the previous day's rain evaporated.

"This is the entrance," Daka announced.

I didn't see any cave or other entrance, but we put down our packs and lit a fire. The brush put out an oily smoke that made our eyes sting. Daka put tobacco in his pipe, along with a bit of a dried healing herb. He measured out a few dried jimson weed seeds into my palm and told me to chew them.

"This will open the pathway," he said. He put the necklace around my neck. "Never take this off, or you may not return."

We solemnly passed the pipe around, each breathing the smoke deep into our lungs.

Suddenly I was alone. It was dark.

"Johnny? Daka?" I could hear no reply. I got to my feet and turned around slowly. I couldn't see anything— Wait. A little light ahead. I groped my way toward it. As I approached, it grew larger. It was grand, made up of many colors, like a solid rainbow ball. I looked down at my hand, and little rainbows of light arched over all of my fingertips. I laughed. Then I retched.

I wiped my mouth and hugged myself, feeling chilled and sick. A large dark spot was forming in the rainbow, coming at me fast. I cried out and ducked. As I looked upward, I saw that it was a great horned owl. I was afraid then, because I knew the owl was the symbol of death.

I felt for my talisman and held it out, saying "I am not dead. I am here to speak to the wolf Sina, leader of the Sawatch Range."

The owl screeched loudly, and the screech turned into deep guttural laughter. I watched, flabbergasted, as the owl transformed into a huge ogre. Filthy, and even scarier than the owl.

"Ha, ha. Is this better, little one? That talisman won't protect you. Normally I would eat you, but you are the Mountain Ma'am. I will help you on your mission— for a price."

"What price?" I asked. I hadn't brought anything with me but the talisman, and Daka had warned me not to part with it.

"A silver coin for payment."

"But I haven't got a silver coin," I said.

"Very well. Sina was buried, but not with a silver coin. So she is not yet in the world of the dead. She is waiting here for admittance, like you."

That was good, as far as I was concerned. "So, can I see her?"

A gray blur appeared in the arch, and Sina walked toward me.

"Sina!"

Hello, Mountain Ma'am.

She was beautiful. Her silver-gray fur shone like the old days, when she was a young pup. I tried not to cry for once.

"Sina, it's not been right without you. I want to bring you back, and all the wolves too." Her gold eyes didn't blink.

We cannot come back, my daughter. Soon all the wolves who ran through our mountains will be gone from our range, and those wolves can never return. And if any were to return against the laws, their descendants would be wiped from the earth.

"But, what if I give you this talisman?" I was willing to die to bring Sina back to life. I took the necklace off and held it out toward her.

No, the talisman is powerless. I know you will find another way to help the wolves.

"How can I, if you're all dead?" I cried. Stubbornly, I reached out for her, and she snarled and snapped at me.

"You bit me!"

You can do this, Mountain Ma'am. Go now. Without payment, I will wait 100 years for admittance, as my ancestors have done.

Sobbing, I slipped the rock back over my head. The rattlesnake was right—why had I come to Wyoming in the first place? I hung my head and stuck my hands into my dungarees, dejected that I had to go back alone. My fingers touched a hard, round object. I pulled it out. A silver coin! A Morgan silver dollar, too. Lady Liberty was real purty, shining with rainbows all around her.

"Ogre, I've got your coin. Will you take Sina now?"

Grinning, he snatched it out of my fingers. Jist like that, the rainbow door disappeared, along with the best friend I'd had in my whole life.

I don't remember what happened for a while after that, but when I woke up, there was Johnny and Daka looking down at me.

"Johnny, I saw Sina! And she's in the spirit world. There was, like, this fairy portal. . ."

"I gathered that," he said.

"You did? I never actually went into the spirit world. The craziest thing was that I needed a silver coin to buy Sina passage from this world. And one jist appeared in my pocket."

Johnny chuckled. "Well, remember when Daka said we'd be your companions? We didn't see what you saw, but we could hear you. When you said, 'I haven't got a silver coin,' we put one in your pocket. We didn't know what it was for, but we knew you needed it."

"Well, thanks," I said, pulling off the talisman and returning it to Daka. "This thing is worthless, though. I wanted to give it to Sina, but she wouldn't take it. In fact, she bit me." Johnny looked surprised, and pulled out a hankerchiff to wrap up my hand.

"What you wanted was impossible, Mountain Ma'am," Daka repeated. "I am sorry I tricked you. I didn't even know for sure that there actually is a spirit world, until you showed me it must be real. But you will find a new way."

That's what Sina had said too. Though Daka had given me false hope, I could forgive him for that—hell, I was even grateful for it—but I couldn't see what way there could be to save the wolves in our world. If I had succeeded in bringing Sina back, all of her descendants would be wiped from the face of the earth. It looked like wolves were doomed, one ways or the other.

—*Descendants!*

Suddenly I was back in the premonition business. I knew for certain that no wolves would return to Colorado in my lifetime. Yet there was a tendril of possibility that someday Sina's descendants here in Wyoming could be reintroduced to their native home.

Maybe that was why I had come here, to learn that the people who have traditionally lived in a place, the more recent settlers, and the natural world all have a stake in shaping the future of a place. Me, Johnny, Daka, and Sina all represented the balance of those claims.

I'd have my work cut out for me, but it was the only way I had left of truly thanking Sina for all she had done for me. I'd probably never see that Promised Land that old Father Dyer over at the church was always talking about. But now I had hope, and I had the way. I was going to run for the State House.

"Get some shuteye, Mountain Ma'am," Johnny said. "We have a long journey ahead of us." I took his hand and felt my eyes grow heavy. I was so tired that I was a little afraid that if I slept I might never wake up again. But I did.

Say, did I ever show you the scar Sina gave me?

###

This Too Shall Pass

Losing my wolf companion caused me to take a long, hard look at who I was and where I was going. I'd become too comfortable in my role as the Mountain Ma'am, taking on anybody I thought was trying to do harm to my Colorado mountains or the wildlife there. Back then, I had the help of the Laramide Nation, Sina, and her animal allies, so I never thought twice about throwing myself into whatever battle caught my fancy. I always came out on top.

But, you never know what you have until you lose it, right? Even with my handsome husband Johnny's help, I couldn't keep up with all the changes in the high country, most of them for the worse. I had to learn the hard way that Sina wasn't coming back, and that the mountains were no longer mine to rule.

"Well, that's America for you," Johnny said. "There ain't any kings and queens any more, like there is in England."

"Yes," I agreed. "And there's hardly any more wolves here, either. So, I guess that leaves me a plain, ordinary woman, don't it?"

"You still got more gumption than ten women," Johnny said, smiling. "What are you going to do with the rest of your life? Settle down and have some kids?" I wasn't so sure he was kidding.

"I'm thinking of running for the State House," I replied. "The thought just come to me when I was vision questing for Sina and she flat refused to come back to the world of the living. But something's got to be done about the wolves going extinct here."

"That's a fine idea, Red," Johnny said. "I'm pretty sure most of Leadville would vote for you. Practically everyone here's a member of the Populist Party, and we swept the Governor's race."

"It helps that I can vote for myself," I retorted. "Here it is 1893, and it's plain ridiculous that I can run for the State House but most women in America can't vote at all."

"Well, you just add that to the list when you get elected," he said.

***

I went over to my best friend Emmaline O'Malley's to tell her the news. She's the local schoolteacher, and she was always inviting me to talk to the children about things like surviving outdoors in the Rockies and the like.

"That's wonderful, Callie!" Emmaline said. "I'll even make you up some bunting that you can put on the railings at the Lucky Lady. 'Vote Wellborn in '94!' It'll look really festive."

The red, white, and blue bunting was a nice idea, 'cause the 4th of July was coming up, and campaigning would follow soon after for the fall elections.

I walked in the town parade on Independence Day and gave my first speech not long afterwards. A crowd gathered in the street in front of the Lucky Lady, drawn as much by the prospect of free sarsaparilla on a hot day as to see me speechify. I stood right in front of the swinging doors. Anyone wanting to get in was going to have to put up with a little bit of my politicking first.

I was in the middle of a spiel about how we were all stewards of the earth and how if they sent me to the State House, I'd do my best to protect both people and the land. I didn't go on too much about animals, because some folks might have thought I was crazy or too sentimental. I wasn't sure how much of the speech anybody heard, since the firecrackers were going off like gatling guns all day.

The crowd parted and then closed again as a young woman with dark hair pushed her way to the front. She was dressed oddly for a girl, with a flat-brimmed straw hat and heavy gray vest with oversize pockets and green trousers. She stood looking at me, a solemn expression on her face. I wondered why someone so young was interested in the campaign but thought maybe it was one of Emmaline's former students, sent to help thicken up the attendance. She looked real interested, though, and I found myself talking straight to her half the time.

Afterwards, Johnny said, "That was a good speech, hon. I noticed you had an admirer in the crowd, too."

"Oh, really?" I said, knowing all along he was talking about the girl in the front row.

"You mean you didn't notice that girl who kept cheering and clapping after every sentence? She really whipped up the crowd. Say, maybe we can get her to help on the campaign. She's young, energetic..."

"And attractive?" I finished. Johnny grinned.

"I jist can't put anything over on you, can I, darlin'?"

"You've still got that wolf inside," I teased.

We didn't see the girl after that, though, and we soon forgot the idea of recruiting her to campaign.

That summer and into the fall, I went door-to-door all over Lake County, drummin' up votes anywhere I could.

I arrived home late one evening, all tuckered out. Johnny sat reading the newspaper and shaking his head.

"What's wrong?" I asked.

"The government's repealed the Sherman Silver Purchase Act," he replied. All the silver barons have gone bust. Leadville's in for it now."

"It's a good thing Horace and Baby Doe already moved to Denver," I said.

"There's a panic on, and it says here they've lost their entire fortune." I could hardly imagine it.

"Maybe they'll find something else they can mine," I said, although I never cared that much about mining. It wasn't something a woman could turn her hand to, and it always made me mad when they said women were bad luck.

In the following weeks, droves of people left, dragging and carrying loads of possessions down Harrison Street. If it got too heavy to carry, they just left it.

Business at the Lucky Lady didn't seem to suffer, though Johnny's General Store lost a lot of its regulars.

There was nothing to do but keep knocking on doors.

One woman answered the door to her cabin and frowned when she saw me.

"A vote for me is a vote for the people and resources of Lake County," I started in. My usual song and dance.

"Get off our place," a man's voice said. A rifle barrel poked over the woman's shoulder.

"My husband's lost his job, so we won't be here to vote," she said. "He's been at your saloon all day drinking. Stop it, John." She pushed the rifle off to the side.

I beat a hasty retreat, grateful that he hadn't recognized me but that she had.

***

Two weeks after election day, the results still weren't final. The first tally showed I was ahead, but the Republicans were putting up a stink about the ballots, so it went to a recount.

"Don't worry, Red," Johnny said. "You won fair and square. Folks appreciated that somebody walked the high country to earn their votes."

But the case dragged on, until late January, when it was almost time for the State General Assembly to convene. The county clerk, Rafer Gardner, kept citing "irregularities" in the voting and declining to make a final decision. Then, a box of ballots was found behind the pew at the church that had somehow gotten "lost." When those got counted, there was no longer any doubt. I later learned Rafer was a Republican and wondered if the lost ballot box was one of the irregularities he talked about. It was a good thing old man Lock was dead, I thought. He would've tried to buy off everybody in sight to get rid of me. Until his dying day, he resented that I'd left his no-good son Harry and remarried. 'A course, there was the little matter of Harry's mysterious death. But my conscience was clear as spring water.

So, finally, I'd gotten elected. I was going to the State House, though I didn't look forward to crossing the twisty, treacherous Loveland Pass in the height of winter. I was packing my bags when the doorpull rang.

"Congratulations, Miz Wellborn." It was the girl who made such an impression on my first day of campaigning. She wore the same wide-brim hat, though now it was winter it was made of wool felt.

"Well, hello, long time no see. What's your name, girl, and where did you come from?" I asked, glancing down the street with snow piled 10 feet high on either side.

"My name's Sarah Summers, and I'm from over in the TenMile Range," she said.

"Well, thank you, Sarah. I'm grateful for your help and support, but I'm runnin' short of time and need to be getting ready to leave Leadville. I'm headed for Denver at last."

Sarah cocked her head slightly, as if listening.

"They wanted me to tell you. . . All of us wish you the best, Mountain Ma'am."

I nearly dropped my suitcase on my foot. But by the time I blinked, she was gone.

***

I squeaked into the city just in time to see the construction of the new Capitol building. It didn't have the fancy gold-plated dome yet—just copper—but it was impressive to me. Leadville had the fancy opera house, but this was much bigger. They were even calling Denver the "Paris of the West" and were expanding the big park in the middle as part of the "City Beautiful" movement that started at the Chicago World's Fair. They were going to fill it with crabapple trees and white lilac bushes come spring.

"I'm going to need a new wardrobe, Johnny." I'd ridden down by horseback, but I was anxious to try one of those new-fangled bicycles to get around town.

I went down to the Denver Dry Goods Company and got myself one of those shorter skirts and a tailored shirt with ruffles at the shoulders and a wool necktie.

"You look like a lady business woman now," Johnny said. "I'm not sure I like it."

"You'll get used to it," I said. "Fashions always start out looking ugly."

I bundled up in a heavy coat and topped it off with a warm felt hat. Unfortunately, tight corsets were still around underneath it all.

"Well, it's practical, I guess," he replied. "Look, I got us matching bicycles. I'm going to ride you over to the State House every day."

"Do you miss the general store?"

"Kind of. But it's exciting being in a big city like this for a change. While you were shopping there, I heard the Denver Dry is looking for a new partner, so I might buy in once we get settled."

***

Arriving early, I kissed Johnny goodbye and climbed the broad staircase in front of the new State Capitol building, made of Colorado white granite. The interior felt only slightly warmer than the frigid January morning. The floors were still being finished, and were of a beautiful rose marble, dusty from their journey from the quarries in the mountains. The smell of fresh paint hung in the air. I gawked up at the rotunda, my mouth hanging open like any tourist, which is how I felt. The lobby opened off to an elegant room, furnished with curved rows of large desks, the Representatives' chamber. Working my way across the rows, I finally found a sign with my name on a desk near the front. I took a seat and waited for more of my new colleagues to arrive.

At first, it seemed like everyone seemed to know each other, but there were some others there who looked equally lost. I got up and asked one where he was from.

"Ouray, in the south," he said. "We're mostly famous for our hot springs."

"Another mountain person. Pleased to meet you," I said, holding out my hand.

The pounding of a gavel signaled the beginning of the session.

At least I'd met one new friend. There was even another woman. I'd make a special effort to meet her tomorrow.

The chairman called for the roll, and I tried my best to remember all the new names, but it was useless. A page circulated around the room, handing out sheets containing the list of bills for the day.

"I'd like to introduce a bill," I whispered to the secretary at the close of the day.

"Well, you'd better get it in quick," he replied. "All the bills are due in the first week." Shocked, I went home to burn the midnight oil. Two days later, I turned in my proposal and settled in to wait for it to rise to the top of the agenda.

***

In late February, there it was, my bill. I exhaled and clasped the day's list to my chest.

The chairman struck his gavel. "House Bill number 66 is next up."

95

Nervous as a wet hen, I stood and was recognized.

"Mr. Chairman, I'd like to introduce House Bill number 66, entitled, 'Protection of Endangered Large Species.'"

"Do you want to make a statement about the bill?" the chairman asked.

"Thank you, Mr. Chairman. As you all know, this bill is aimed at protecting Lobo wolves, which 'most everyone calls gray wolves. They have big, bushy tails and weigh upwards of 80 pounds. They are an important part of the wildlife of Colorado, and they keep animals like deer and rabbits in check. They're important to the culture of our Indian population too. It's a little-known fact that the Indians hereabouts are descended from Asiatics that came over the land bridge crossing the Bering Strait into Alaska. They bred their domesticated dogs with wolves and coyotes to get the animals you see today. Before the white man brought horses, Lobo wolves were used as pack animals. So, as you can see, the recent drive to eradicate them is really harming a potentially useful animal."

"Mr. Chairman!" A lanky cowboy interrupted. I wondered why nobody'd told him to take off his hat.

"The chair recognizes the representative from Salida."

"I'm a rancher, and we don't have any use for wolves, gray, green, or otherwise," the cowboy said. Loud cheering erupted, and he sat back down.

"Mr. Chairman," I said. "Wolves may look ferocious, but they are not ferocious, even those that have lived in the wilds. Those tales you hear about the big bad wolf are just that—tales. Poison, traps, and guns just aren't necessary, because there's so few of them left."

"Just as long as they stay off my ranch, I won't shoot 'em," the cowboy said. More laughing.

"That's just it," I replied, feeling a little heat under the collar of my lady business blouse. "They don't know where your ranch begins and ends. They need a large area to hunt in. They might go up to thirty miles a night following game—or even more—and be back before dawn."

"I don't want wolves anywhere on my ranch," the cowboy retorted. "At the least, they upset the cattle."

The debate continued all morning, until the Chairman called for a vote.

It was 50-14 against.

***

"I guess I ain't very persuasive," I groused afterward. "If I had Sina by my side, she would have made that cowboy see sense."

"I don't see Sina sitting quietly at your side wearing a leash," Johnny said. "Unless you had her stuffed. . . What are you going to do next?"

"I can always wait until next year and reintroduce my bill, but the wolves' time is running out. Maybe I can take it to the courts."

"Well, it's an idea," Johnny agreed. "Most of the legislature is made up of farmers and ranchers, and a few rich lawyers. A sympathetic judge might see things different. By the way, Cal, I've got a surprise that might cheer you up." He flashed two tickets.

"Some kind of show, like the opera?" I guessed.

"It's Buffalo Bill's Wild West Show," Johnny said. "They're just back from touring all over Europe."

***

I kind of disapproved of Buffalo Bill. He was famous for winning a bet about who could shoot the most bison out the windows while riding a train across the plains. And bison had been one of the main foods for wolves. But I thoroughly enjoyed the show, especially all the sharp shooting.

"I shore wish I could have shot my Sharps that good," I said, as the crowd cheered Annie Oakley and Frank Butler's act.

"I think you could've given them a run for their money," Johnny noted. "Probably still can."

"Flatterer." Johnny leaned over and kissed me on the cheek.

Buffalo Bill stepped to the center of the arena.

"Ladies and gentlemen. We have the honor of having in our audience one of the first ladies of Leadville, Mrs. Callie Wellborn, recently elected to the State House of Representatives. Would you please stand?"

I rose, my cheeks reddening. "Did you put him up to this, Johnny?"

"He met royalty in Europe. Why not here at home? You *are* the Mountain Ma'am, after all."

Addressing the crowd, Buffalo Bill added, "We thank you for your work to save our wild species, in the high parks, Mrs. Wellborn. We hear the furnishings down at the new State House are a little sparse, so to help, the Wild West Show is donating one of my rifles and a buffalo pelt to hang in the rotunda."

I nodded and sat down, to scattered applause.

"Thanks very much, your lordship," I muttered.

***

"I'm afraid you're fighting a losing battle right now, Mrs. Wellborn," Judge Murphy said. "I know they were a big part of the natural landscape before the white man came, but now the lack of food for the wolves brought about by the destruction of bison, elk, deer, and smaller animals is almost certainly going to lead to their extinction. I'm sorry. I really am. But I can't overturn the legislature's vote. At the most, all I could do is declare a law to be unconstitutional, and you never got anything passed in the first place. But one thing you *did* do is educate some folks.

"If I'm any judge of history, I think the wolves will come back some day. Things tend to go in cycles, especially in nature. And you did mention that you've seen the wolves are doing okay up in Wyoming, right? The more people see that they are useful animals, the more chance they will be allowed back in Colorado."

"Thank you, judge. You've been real helpful, even if it is only to give me a little hope. Well, I won't take up more of your valuable time."

"You're quite welcome, and remember, there's always next year."

I left the judge's office and crossed back over Colfax Avenue to the Capitol building.

Workmen were hanging up the rifle and buffalo hide donated by Buffalo Bill along the south hallway.

The foreman tipped his cap. "Afternoon, Mrs. Wellborn."

"Do you mind if I touch it?" I asked.

He glanced around. "Why sure. It's a big, wooly old thing, ain't it?"

I reached out and gently stroked the pelt. Life seemed to flow out of it and into me, and I understood the animal's sacrifice. But the feeling was not as strong as it been had that day when as a girl I wrapped a grizzly bear rug around my shoulders, stole my worthless husband's rifle, and headed out into the snowy mountains of Colorado.

***

It was one of the best kisses ever, and Johnny and I had lots of practice.

"Happy New Year, hon," Johnny said. "It's hard to believe it's 1933, ain't it? And that we lasted this long?"

"It sure is. I don't know how we got so old all of a sudden."

"You ain't old, Red," Johnny said. "And neither am I. We've still got that spark. The lights are still up at the Civic Center. Do you want to walk over and see them?"

"I'm up for it. Let's see if Ron wants to come with us."

I knocked on Ron's door. Our son was visiting during the Christmas break from the university. Our pride and joy, Ron was a Biology professor at the University of Colorado in Boulder, but still a bachelor, much to my dismay. We'd argued about it a few times, but he always countered with, "I just haven't found the right girl—I'll know her when I see her." But at least there was a chance.

"I'd like to see this year's lights," Ron said. "They get fancier every year. How long have they been doing them?"

"Your mother might know that," Johnny said. "What is it? Five years?"

"Since nineteen twenty-six," I said. "I helped collect the donations to get it started. They'll leave them up through the Stock Show."

"Well, they're always beautiful, Mom," Ron said, hugging me.

We were in the middle of piling on coats, scarves, and boots when the doorbell rang.

"Now, who could that be at this time of night?" I wondered aloud.

"Probably some drunk, out celebratin' and lost his keys," Johnny said.

I opened the door, and a blast of icy air shouldered its way into the living room.

A young woman in flat-brimmed wool hat and gray uniform coat stood on the landing. I switched on the porch light. Dark hair fell to her shoulders, and long, dark lashes framed gold eyes. She looked familiar somehow.

"Mrs. Wellborn? You may not remember me. My name is Sarah Summers. I work for the National Park Service. We met recently during the rally to keep the last few wolves from going extinct."

"Come in, girl. Now I remember. You know, you look just like a girl from the TenMile Range who helped us when I ran for Congress. Johnny and I waited for you, wonderin' where you'd got to... But, land sakes, that's got to have been over thirty years ago, now. It couldn't have been you. I get confused a lot lately."

Sarah smiled and shook her head. "No, but I do work in the TenMile Range. I'm just here to remind you that I'll drop by tomorrow to take you to visit the area where a wolf might have been spotted. You promised to come, remember?"

"Johnny, look who's here," I said. "Damned if it isn't the next Mountain Ma'am." Another thought struck me.

"Sarah, have you met my son Ron?"

It's never too late to hope, I always say.

*****~~~~~*****

Afterword: The Wolf in Colorado

The wolf has long inspired fear in imagination and in reality. In Europe, packs of wolves were known to attack horses, livestock, and even people in carriages. Willa Cather tells a particularly frightening fictional tale in *My Antonia*. Robert Browning's poem, "Ivan Ivanovitch" has a mother tossing her children one by one to pursuing wolves. Even as recently as 2013, northern Russia declared a state of emergency after a "super pack" of 400 wolves laid siege to the remote town of Verkhoyansk. But some dismiss such tales, saying wild dogs are more likely responsible. Most such stories are probably a mixture.

But we are not talking about European timber wolves when we talk about the wolf in Colorado. The wolves in Colorado in the 1800s, like our character, Sina, were Canadian in origin. Native American tribes of the Plains, such as the Pawnee, actually admired and identified with wolves, calling themselves the "Wolf People."

As Callie Dawson-Wellborn explains in her campaign in "This Too Shall Pass," she seeks to protect a variety of Mexican Gray Wolf, nicknamed "El Lobo" (*Canis lupus baileyi*). They were relatively small, peaceful predators compared to their feared European cousins. Yet Callie's crusade to save them falls on deaf ears. By the

1930s, these wolves were extinct throughout the United States. Though they still exist in scattered habitats, they are listed as an endangered species.

There are now efforts to restore wolves to their former natural range. After being wiped out in the United States and with only a few animals remaining in Mexico, Mexican gray wolves were bred in captivity and reintroduced to the wild in Arizona beginning in 1998. Once the top predator in the borderlands, biologists believe that once lobos return to healthy numbers, they will restore balance to the Southwest's ecosystems by keeping deer, elk, and javelina populations healthy and in check. But it will take many more years before that happens.

Similarly, Canadian wolves are being introduced in the northern U.S., including Yellowstone National Park, Wyoming, Idaho, Montana, and New Mexico. Proposals have been made to restore wolves to wilderness ecosystems of Colorado, where they could provide a natural check on populations of elk, for example. The suggestions have met with considerable opposition from some ranchers, however. Reports of a possible wolf sighting in Colorado have been made as recently as 2007, according to the Colorado Department of Parks and Wildlife.

So, keep your eyes peeled. It's possible that someday, like Callie, you may spot a wild wolf. Treat her with caution, and above all, with respect.

More Reading: "Lobo, the King of Currumpa," in *Wild Animals I Have Known*, 1898, Ernest Thompson Seton. Available (in the public domain) via Project Gutenberg. http://www.gutenberg.org/ebooks/3031

*****~~~~~*****

About the Author

Juliana Rew is a former science and technical writer for the National Center for Atmospheric Research and the Geological Society of America. She has won over a dozen technical writing competitions, and is a software engineer by training. She also publishes fantasy and science fiction stories by other authors at Third Flatiron Publishing. For more information about her books, visit her author website, www.julianarew.com.

*****~~~~~*****

Acknowledgments and Art Credits

Ebook only:

"Mountain Ma'am" - Keely Rew

"Family Matters" - Prospectors in Pikes Peak region of Colorado, ca. 1858. Wikimedia Commons file, taken from Alpenrose website, http://www.alpenrosepress.com/images/Recen.jpg, uploaded by William McLaurin

"Raised by Wolves" - Juliana Rew

"Skunks versus Woodpeckers" - Skunk diorama, Denver Museum of Nature & Science; Wikimedia Commons file: Arizona woodpecker female by Alan Wilson, http://naturespicsonline.com

"Whalebone Corset" - Wikimedia Commons file: Lady's corset, 1882 Harper's Bazaar.

"Doc Frain" - Oberon, king of the fairies in "A Midsummer Night's Dream," by William Shakespeare, played by Victor Jory (1935 film)

Juliana Rew

"The Chimera and the Coin" - Wikimedia Commons file, *Canis lupus* photograph by Martin Mecnarowski, http://www.photomecan.eu/

*****~~~~~*****

Discover other titles by Juliana Rew:

Erenarch Academy: Under the Dragon Banner
Miranda of Daris
Mountain Ma'am

www.julianarew.com

www.ingramcontent.com/pod-product-compliance
Lightning Source LLC
Chambersburg PA
CBHW070502130626
46555CB00003B/1126